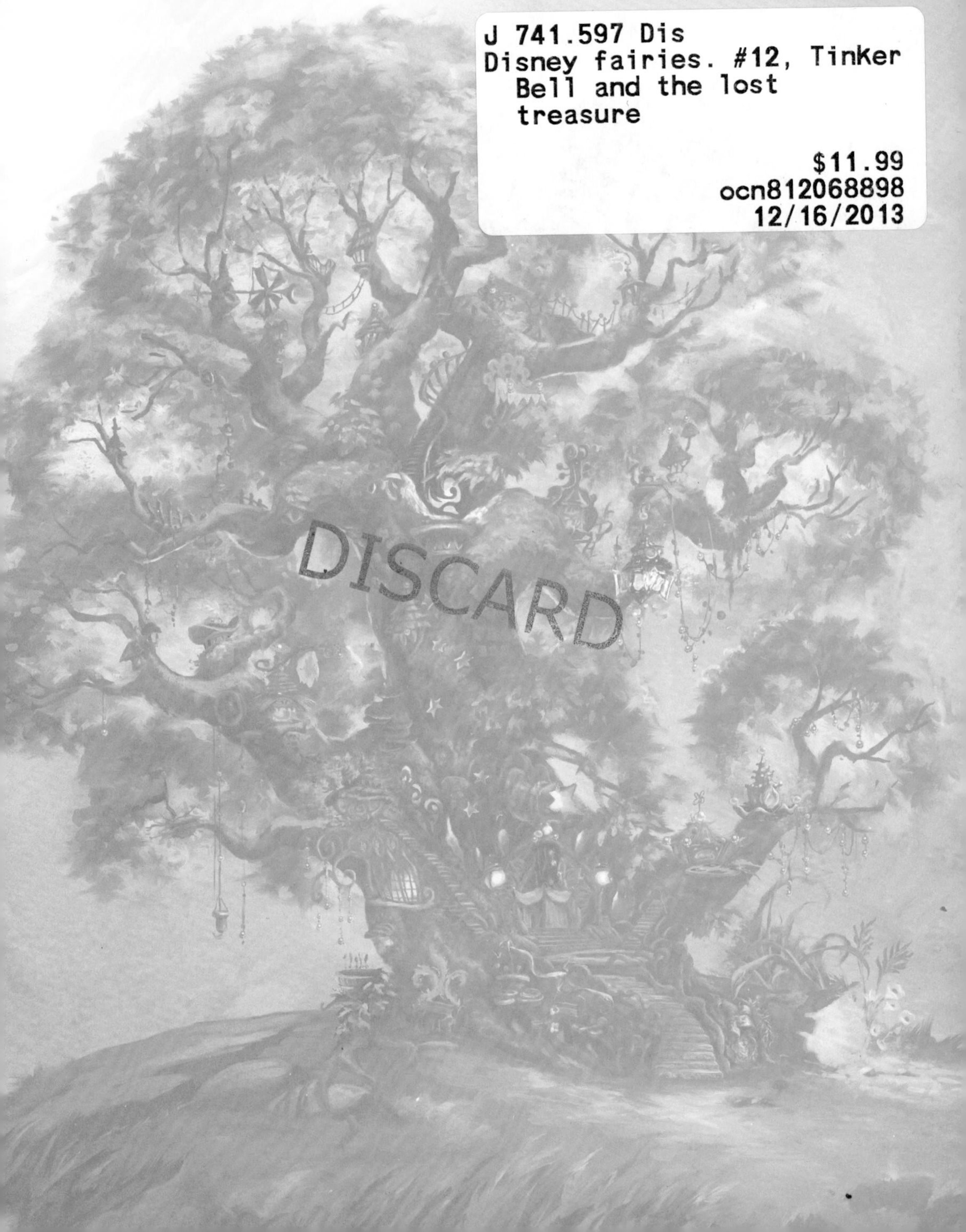

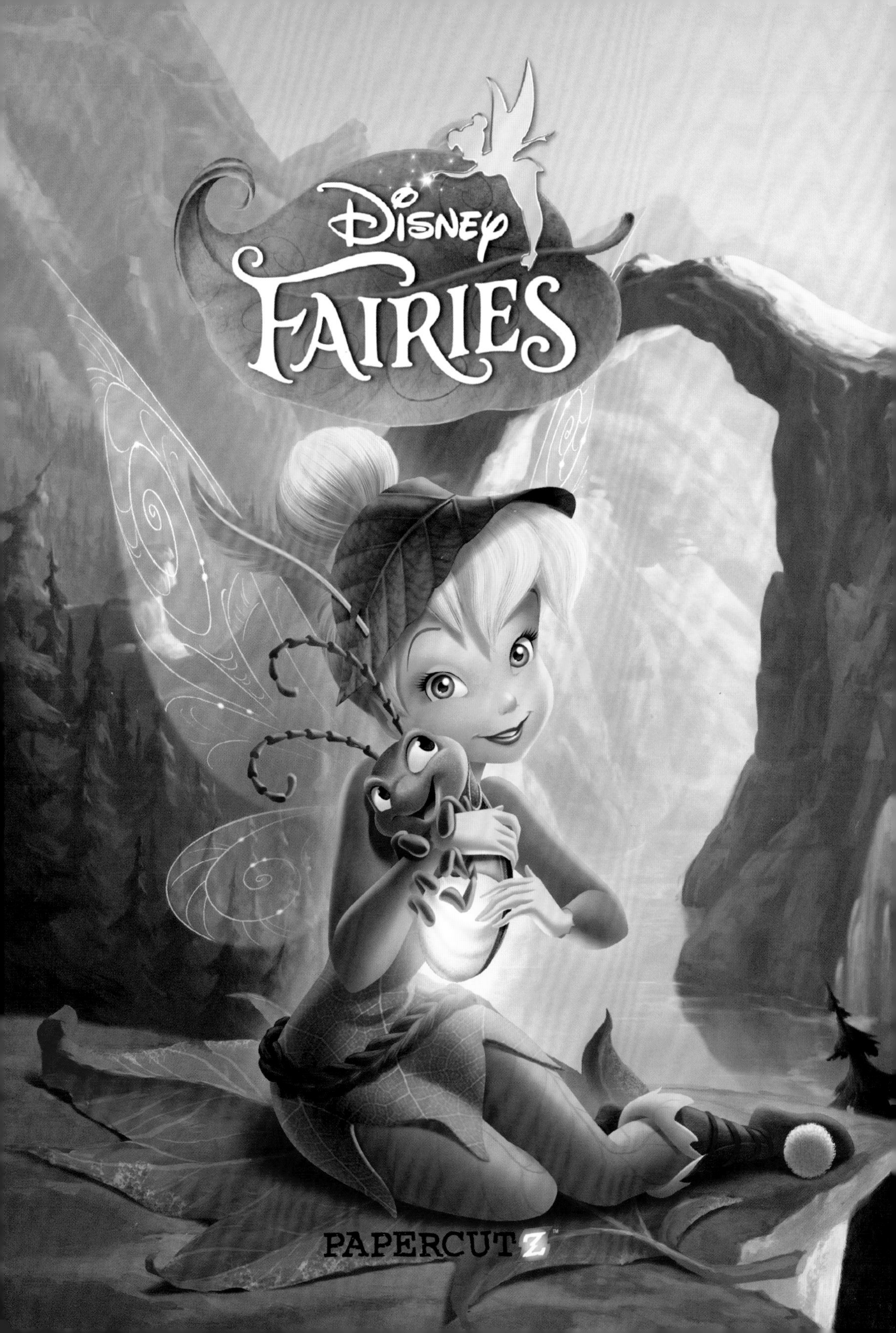
Disney
FAIRIES
PAPERCUTZ

Disney FAIRIES

Graphic Novels Available from
PAPERCUTZ

Graphic Novel #1

"Prilla's Talent"

Graphic Novel #2

"Tinker Bell and the Wings of Rani"

Graphic Novel #3

"Tinker Bell and the Day of the Dragon"

Graphic Novel #4

"Tinker Bell to the Rescue"

Graphic Novel #5

"Tinker Bell and the Pirate Adventure"

Graphic Novel #6

"A Present for Tinker Bell"

Graphic Novel #7

"Tinker Bell the Perfect Fairy"

Graphic Novel #8

"Tinker Bell and her Stories for a Rainy Day"

Graphic Novel #9

"Tinker Bell and her Magical Arrival"

Graphic Novel #10

"Tinker Bell and the Lucky Rainbow"

Coming Soon:

Graphic Novel #11

"Tinker Bell and the Most Precious Gift"

Graphic Novel #12

"Tinker Bell and the Lost Treasure"

Graphic Novel #13

"Tinker Bell and the Pixie Hollow Games"

Tinker Bell and the Great Fairy Rescue

DISNEY FAIRIES graphic novels are available in paperback for $7.99 each;
in hardcover for $12.99 each except #5, $6.99PB, $10.99HC.
#6-13 are $7.99PB $11.99HC. Tinker Bell and the Great Fairy Rescue is $9.99 in hardcover only.
Available at booksellers everywhere.

See more at papercutz.com

Or you can order from us: Please add $4.00 for postage and handling for first book, and add $1.00 for each
additional book. Please make check payable to NBM Publishing. Send to: Papercutz, 160 Broadway, Suite 700, East
Wing, New York, NY 10038 or call 800 886 1223 (9-6 EST M-F) MC-Visa-Amex accepted.

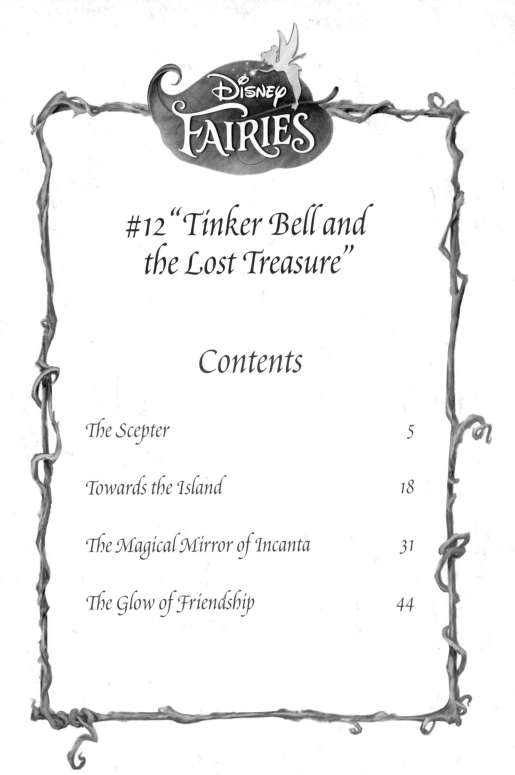

DISNEY FAIRIES

#12 "Tinker Bell and the Lost Treasure"

Contents

PAPERCUTZ™
NEW YORK

"The Scepter"
Concept and Script: Augusto Macchetto
Revised Captions: Cortney Faye Powell
Layout: Denise Shimabukuro
Pencils: Manuela Razzi
Inks: Roberta Zanotta
Color: Studio Kawaii
Letters: Janice Chiang
Page 5 art:
Concept: Tea Orsi
Pencils and Inks: Sara Storino
Color: Andrea Cagol

"The Magical Mirror of Incanta"
Concept and Script: Augusto Macchetto
Revised Captions: Cortney Faye Powell
Layout: Denise Shimabukuro
Pencils: Manuela Razzi
Inks: Roberta Zanotta
Color: Studio Kawaii
Letters: Janice Chiang
Page 31 Art:
Concept: Tea Orsi
Pencils and Inks: Sara Storino
Color: Andrea Cagol

"Towards the Island"
Concept and Script: Augusto Macchetto
Revised Captions: Cortney Faye Powell
Layout: Denise Shimabukuro
Pencils: Manuela Razzi
Inks: Marina Baggio
Color: Studio Kawaii
Letters: Janice Chiang
Page 18 Art:
Concept: Tea Orsi
Pencils and Inks: Sara Storino
Color: Andrea Cagol

"The Glow of Friendship"
Concept and Script: Augusto Macchetto
Revised Captions: Cortney Faye Powell
Layout: Denise Shimabukuro
Pencils: Manuela Razzi
Inks: Roberta Zanotta
Color: Studio Kawaii
Letters: Janice Chiang
Page 44 Art:
Concept: Tea Orsi
Pencils and Inks: Sara Storino
Color: Andrea Cagol

Production – Dawn K. Guzzo
Special Thanks – John Tanzer and Shiho Tilley
Production Coordinator – Beth Scorzato
Associate Editor – Michael Petranek
Jim Salicrup
Editor-in-Chief

ISBN: 978-1-59707-428-5 paperback edition
ISBN: 978-1-59707-429-2 hardcover edition

Printed in China
April 2013 by Asia One Printing LTD
13/F Asia One Tower
8 Fung Yip St., Chaiwan
Hong Kong

Papercutz books may be purchased for business or promotional use.
For information on bulk purchases please contact
Macmillan Corporate and Premium Sales Department at
(800) 221-7945 x5442.

Distributed by Macmillan
First Papercutz Printing

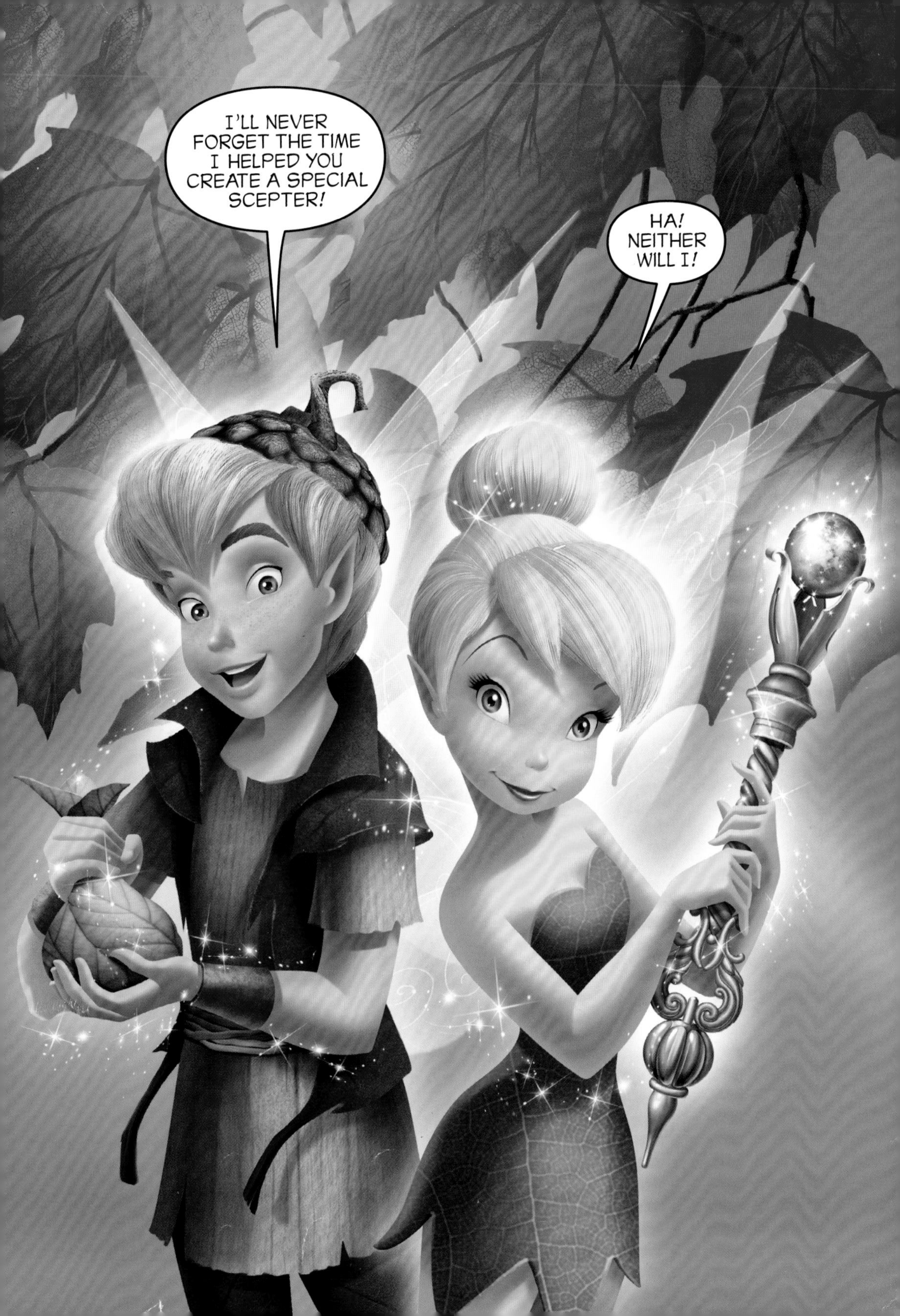
I'LL NEVER FORGET THE TIME I HELPED YOU CREATE A SPECIAL SCEPTER!
HA! NEITHER WILL I!

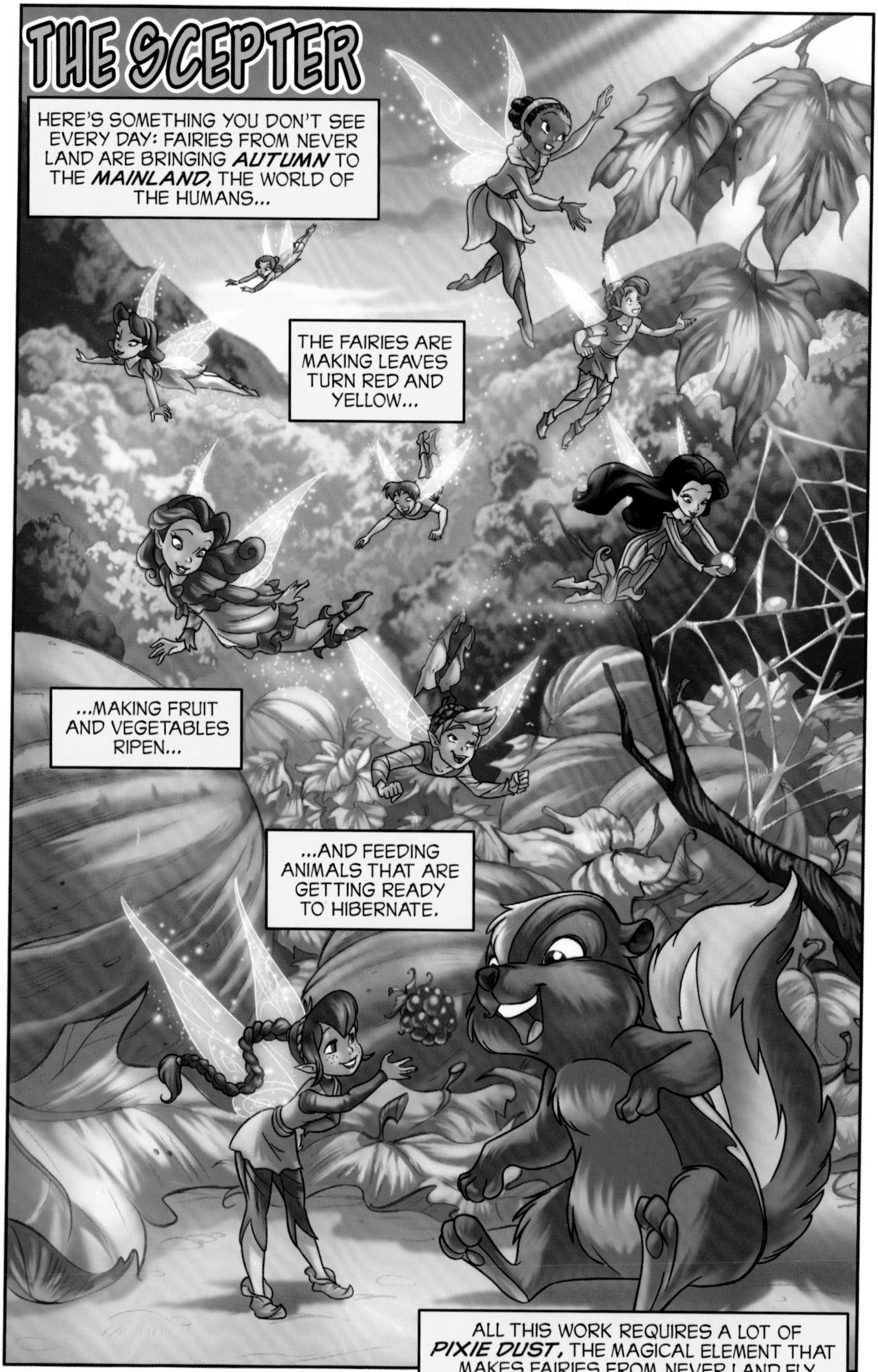
THE SCEPTER
HERE'S SOMETHING YOU DON'T SEE EVERY DAY: FAIRIES FROM NEVER LAND ARE BRINGING *AUTUMN* TO THE *MAINLAND,* THE WORLD OF THE HUMANS...
THE FAIRIES ARE MAKING LEAVES TURN RED AND YELLOW...
...MAKING FRUIT AND VEGETABLES RIPEN...
...AND FEEDING ANIMALS THAT ARE GETTING READY TO HIBERNATE.
ALL THIS WORK REQUIRES A LOT OF *PIXIE DUST,* THE MAGICAL ELEMENT THAT MAKES FAIRIES FROM NEVER LAND FLY.

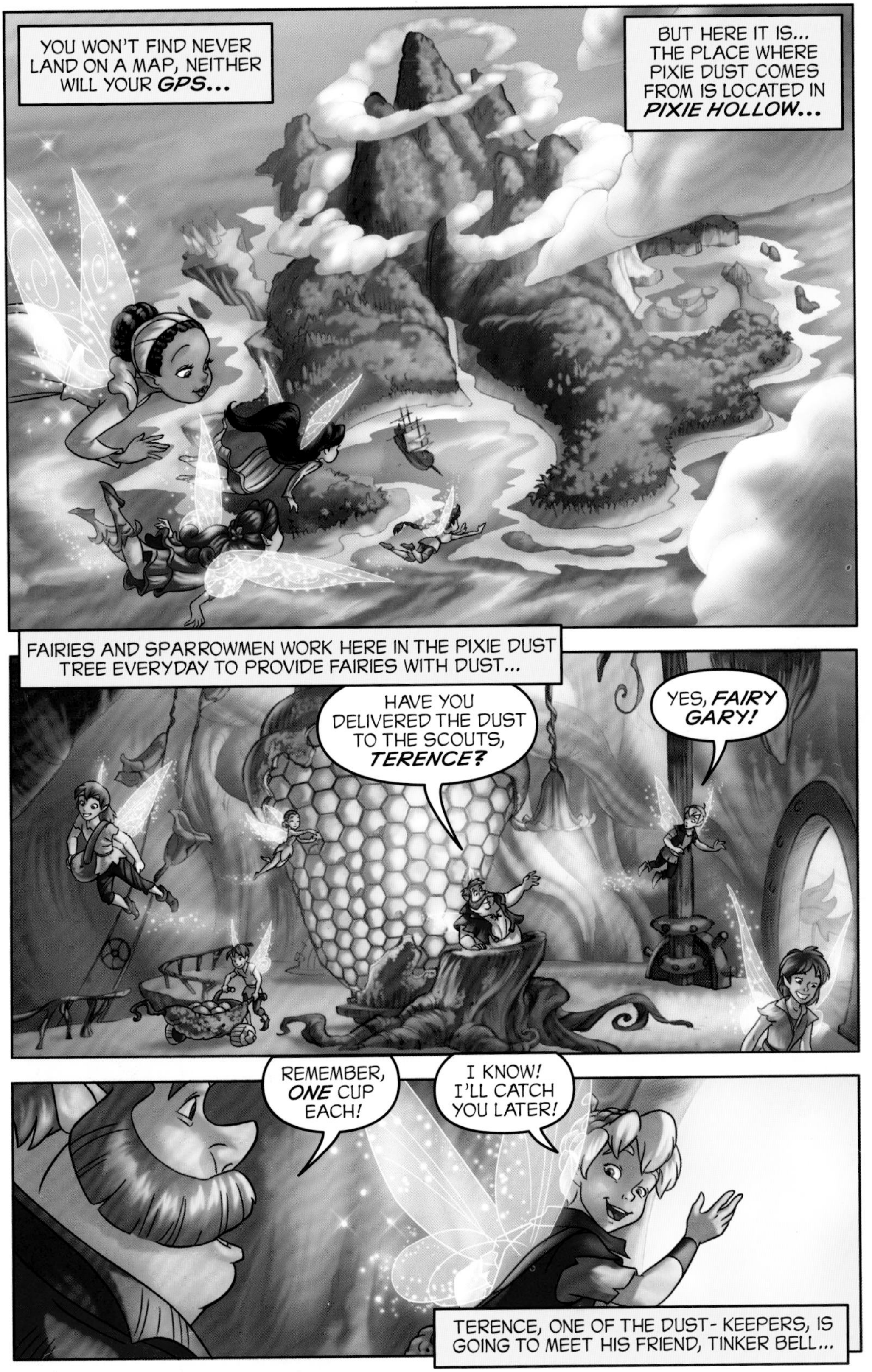

YOU WON'T FIND NEVER LAND ON A MAP, NEITHER WILL YOUR GPS...
BUT HERE IT IS... THE PLACE WHERE PIXIE DUST COMES FROM IS LOCATED IN PIXIE HOLLOW...
FAIRIES AND SPARROWMEN WORK HERE IN THE PIXIE DUST TREE EVERYDAY TO PROVIDE FAIRIES WITH DUST...
HAVE YOU DELIVERED THE DUST TO THE SCOUTS, TERENCE?
YES, FAIRY GARY!
REMEMBER, ONE CUP EACH!
I KNOW! I'LL CATCH YOU LATER!
TERENCE, ONE OF THE DUST- KEEPERS, IS GOING TO MEET HIS FRIEND, TINKER BELL...

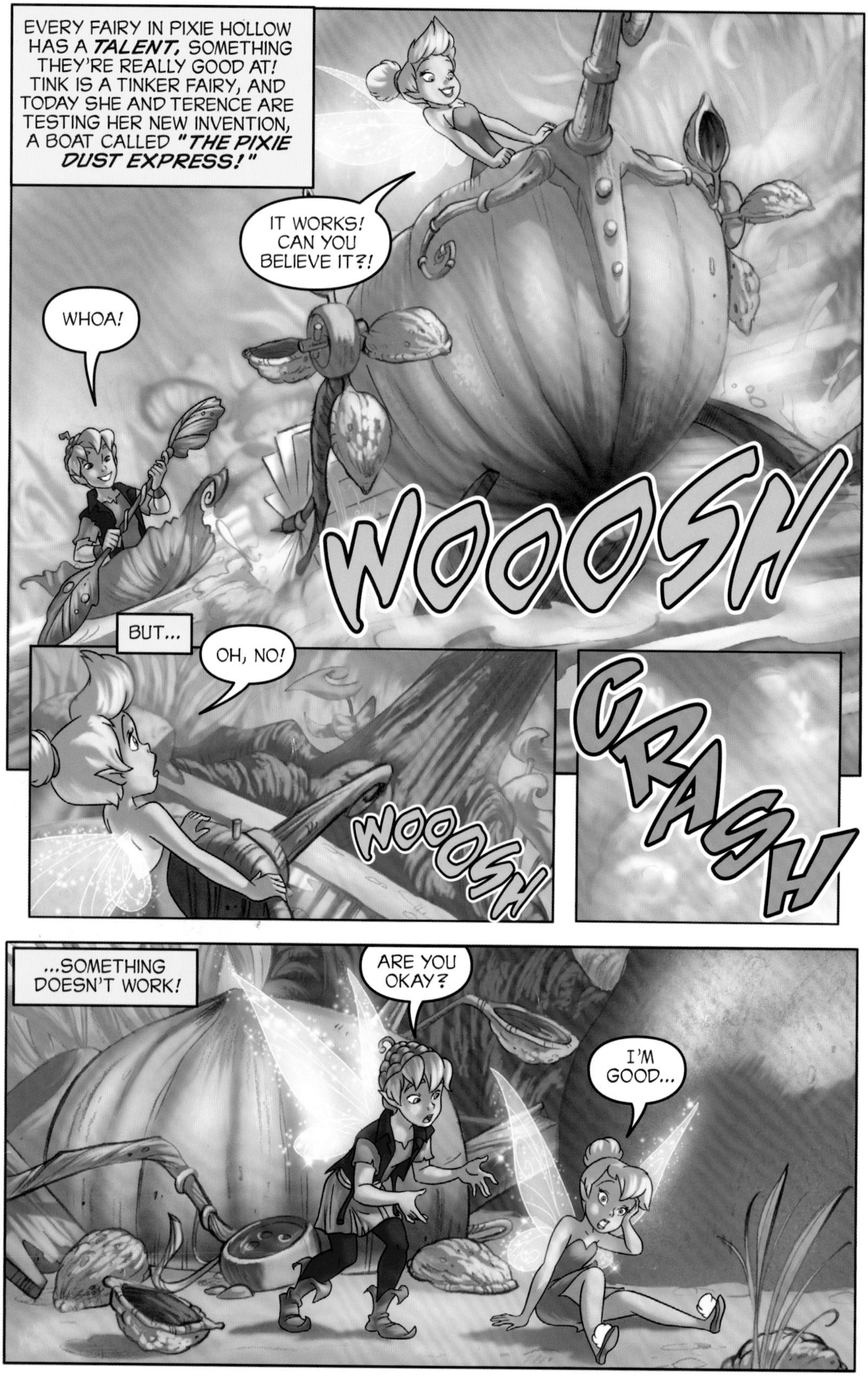
EVERY FAIRY IN PIXIE HOLLOW HAS A ***TALENT,*** SOMETHING THEY'RE REALLY GOOD AT! TINK IS A TINKER FAIRY, AND TODAY SHE AND TERENCE ARE TESTING HER NEW INVENTION, A BOAT CALLED ***"THE PIXIE DUST EXPRESS!"***
IT WORKS! CAN YOU BELIEVE IT?!
WHOA!
WOOOSH
BUT...
OH, NO!
WOOOSH
CRASH
...SOMETHING DOESN'T WORK!
ARE YOU OKAY?
I'M GOOD...

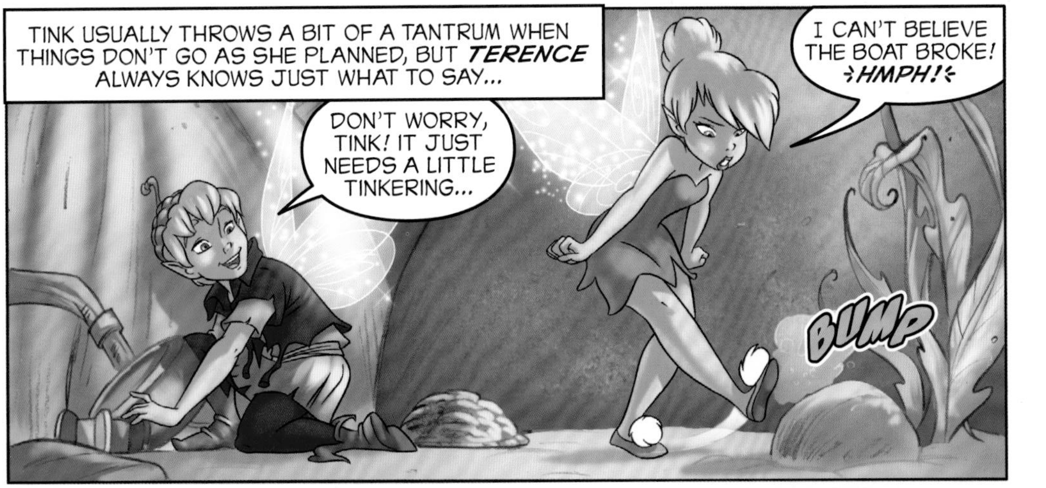
TINK USUALLY THROWS A BIT OF A TANTRUM WHEN THINGS DON'T GO AS SHE PLANNED, BUT *TERENCE* ALWAYS KNOWS JUST WHAT TO SAY...
I CAN'T BELIEVE THE BOAT BROKE! *HMPH!*
DON'T WORRY, TINK! IT JUST NEEDS A LITTLE TINKERING...
BUMP

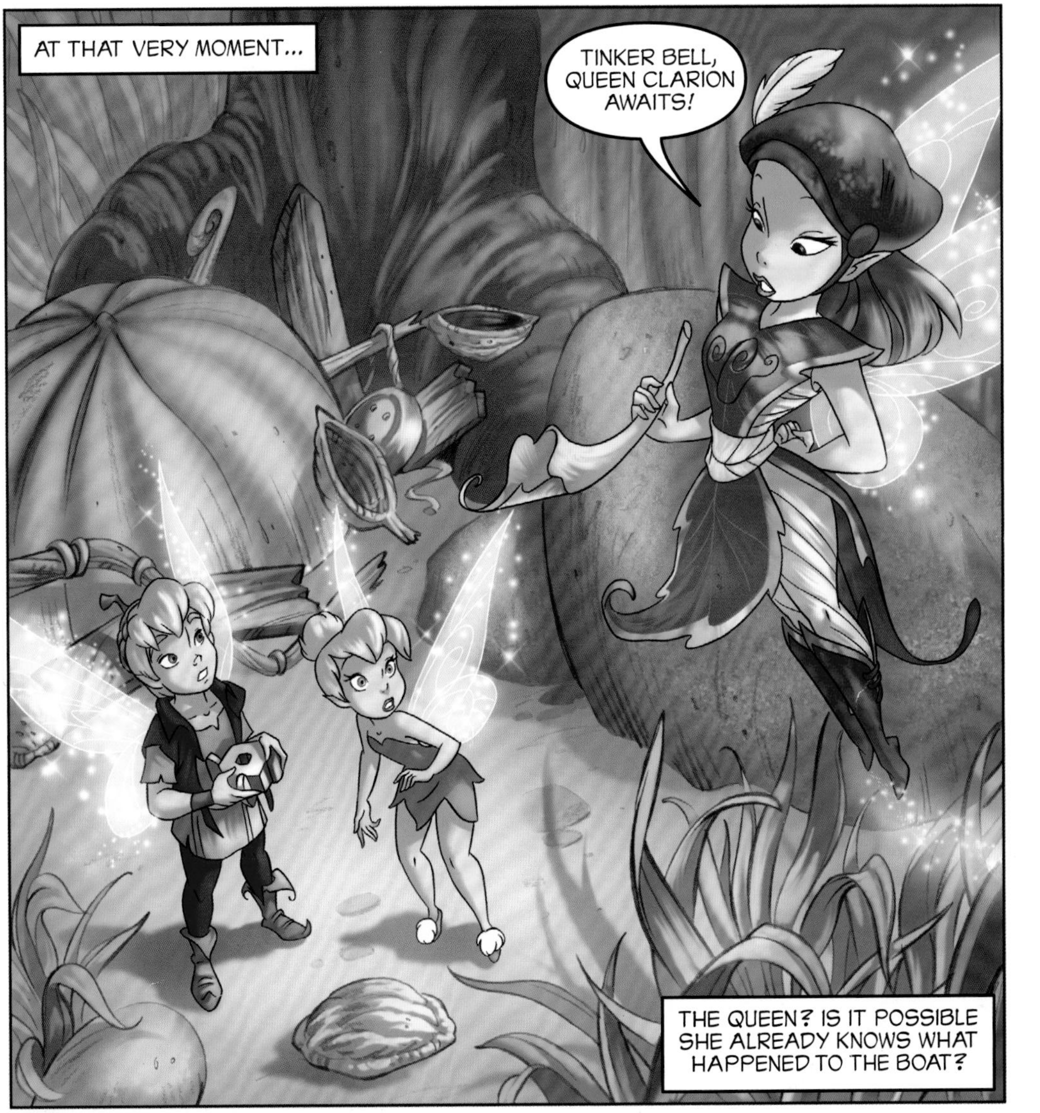
AT THAT VERY MOMENT...
TINKER BELL, QUEEN CLARION AWAITS!
THE QUEEN? IS IT POSSIBLE SHE ALREADY KNOWS WHAT HAPPENED TO THE BOAT?

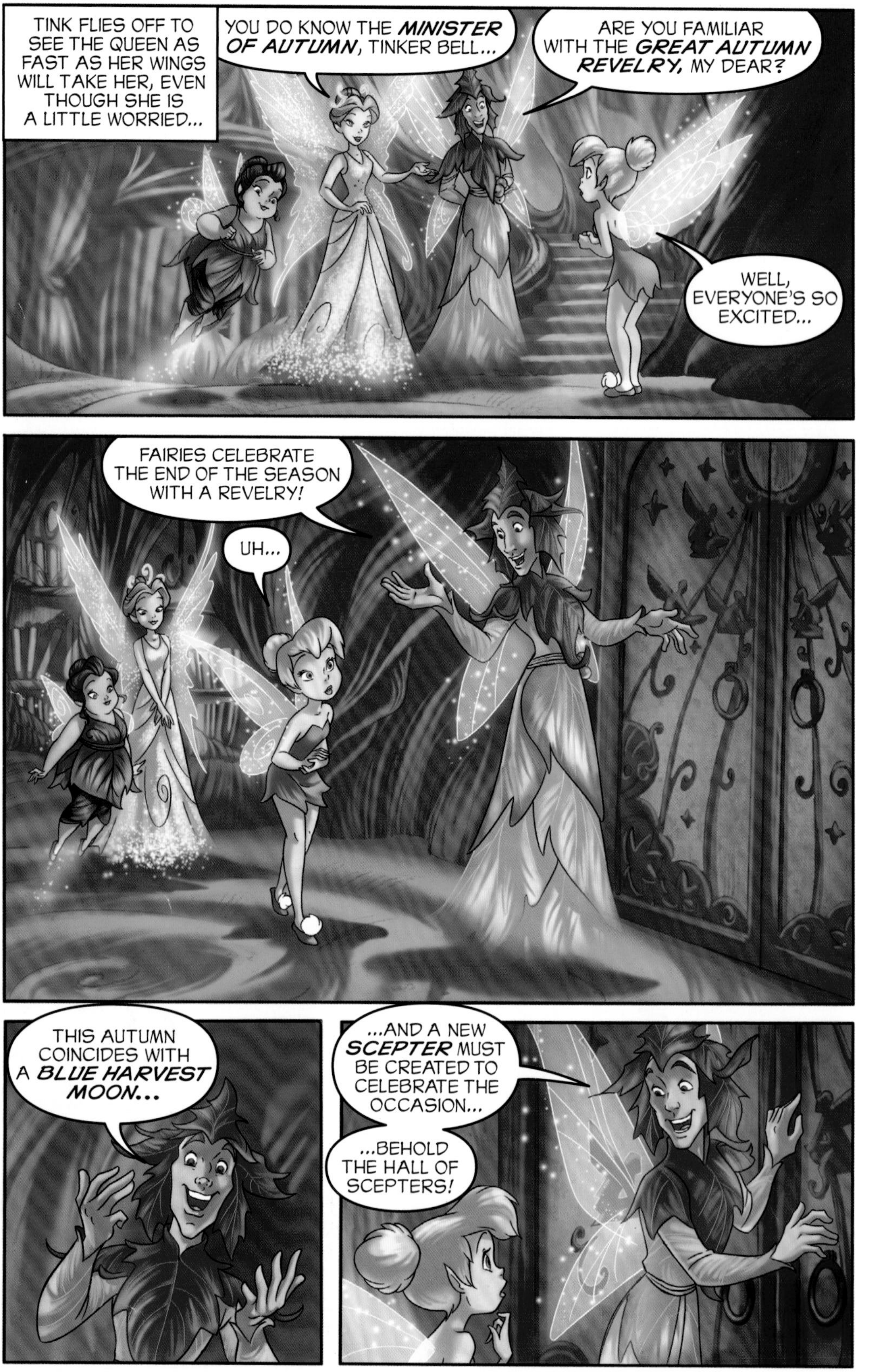
TINK FLIES OFF TO SEE THE QUEEN AS FAST AS HER WINGS WILL TAKE HER, EVEN THOUGH SHE IS A LITTLE WORRIED...
YOU DO KNOW THE ***MINISTER OF AUTUMN***, TINKER BELL...
ARE YOU FAMILIAR WITH THE ***GREAT AUTUMN REVELRY,*** MY DEAR?
WELL, EVERYONE'S SO EXCITED...
FAIRIES CELEBRATE THE END OF THE SEASON WITH A REVELRY!
UH...
THIS AUTUMN COINCIDES WITH A ***BLUE HARVEST MOON...***
...AND A NEW ***SCEPTER*** MUST BE CREATED TO CELEBRATE THE OCCASION...
...BEHOLD THE HALL OF SCEPTERS!

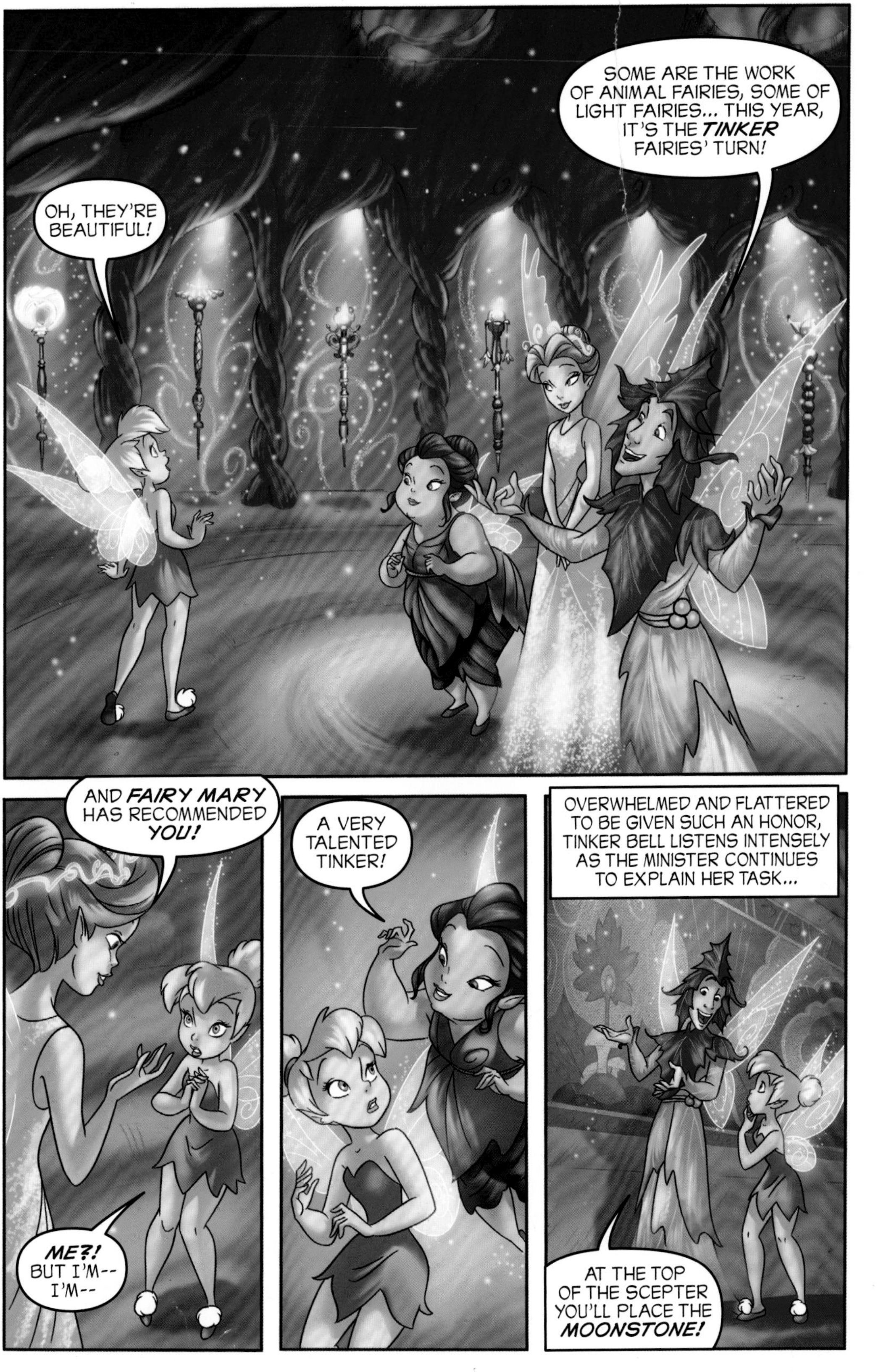
OH, THEY'RE BEAUTIFUL!
SOME ARE THE WORK OF ANIMAL FAIRIES, SOME OF LIGHT FAIRIES... THIS YEAR, IT'S THE *TINKER* FAIRIES' TURN!
AND *FAIRY MARY* HAS RECOMMENDED *YOU!*
ME?! BUT I'M-- I'M--
A VERY TALENTED TINKER!
OVERWHELMED AND FLATTERED TO BE GIVEN SUCH AN HONOR, TINKER BELL LISTENS INTENSELY AS THE MINISTER CONTINUES TO EXPLAIN HER TASK...
AT THE TOP OF THE SCEPTER YOU'LL PLACE THE *MOONSTONE!*

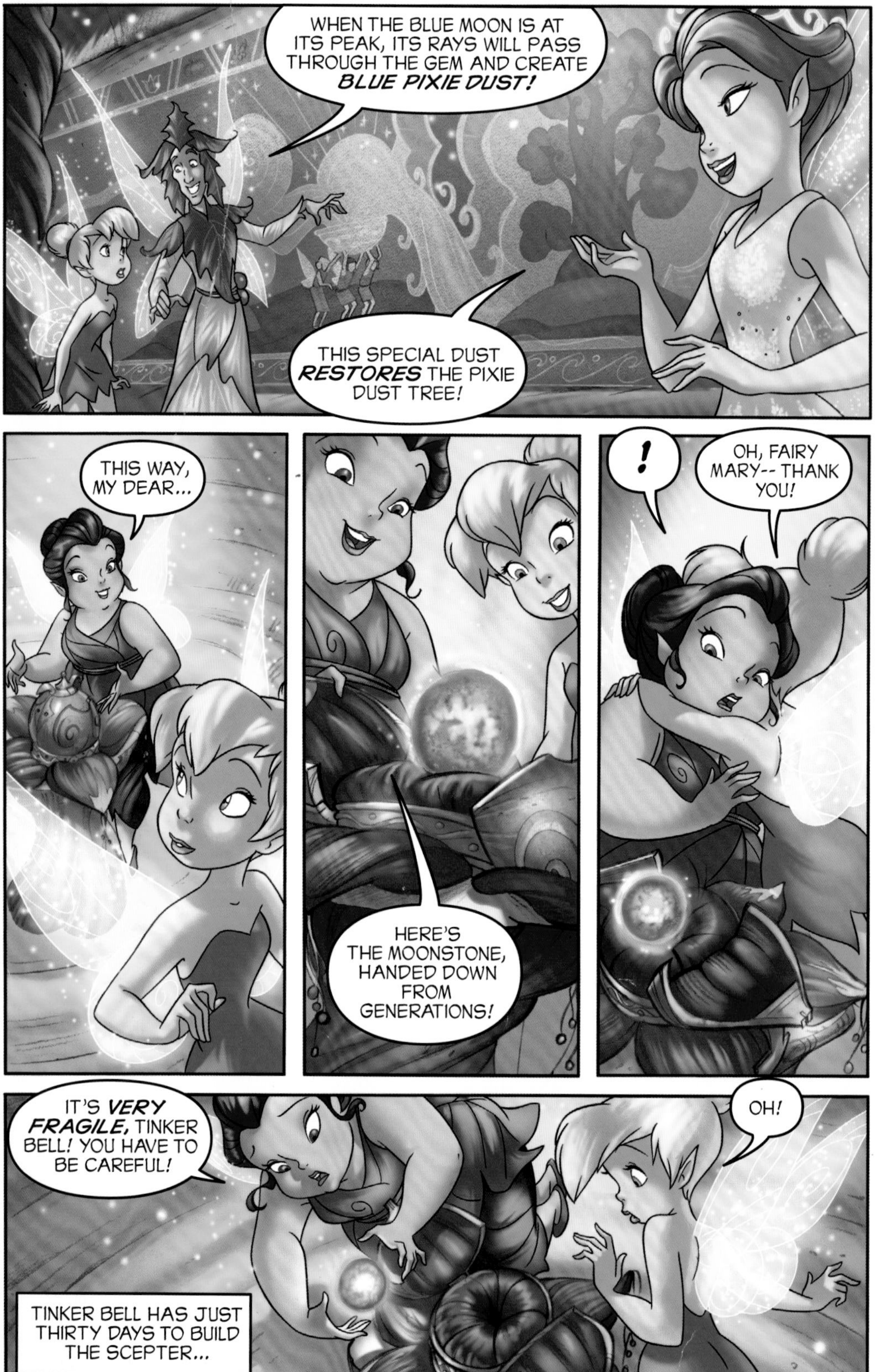
WHEN THE BLUE MOON IS AT ITS PEAK, ITS RAYS WILL PASS THROUGH THE GEM AND CREATE *BLUE PIXIE DUST!*
THIS SPECIAL DUST *RESTORES* THE PIXIE DUST TREE!
THIS WAY, MY DEAR...
HERE'S THE MOONSTONE, HANDED DOWN FROM GENERATIONS!
!
OH, FAIRY MARY-- THANK YOU!
IT'S *VERY FRAGILE,* TINKER BELL! YOU HAVE TO BE CAREFUL!
OH!
TINKER BELL HAS JUST THIRTY DAYS TO BUILD THE SCEPTER...

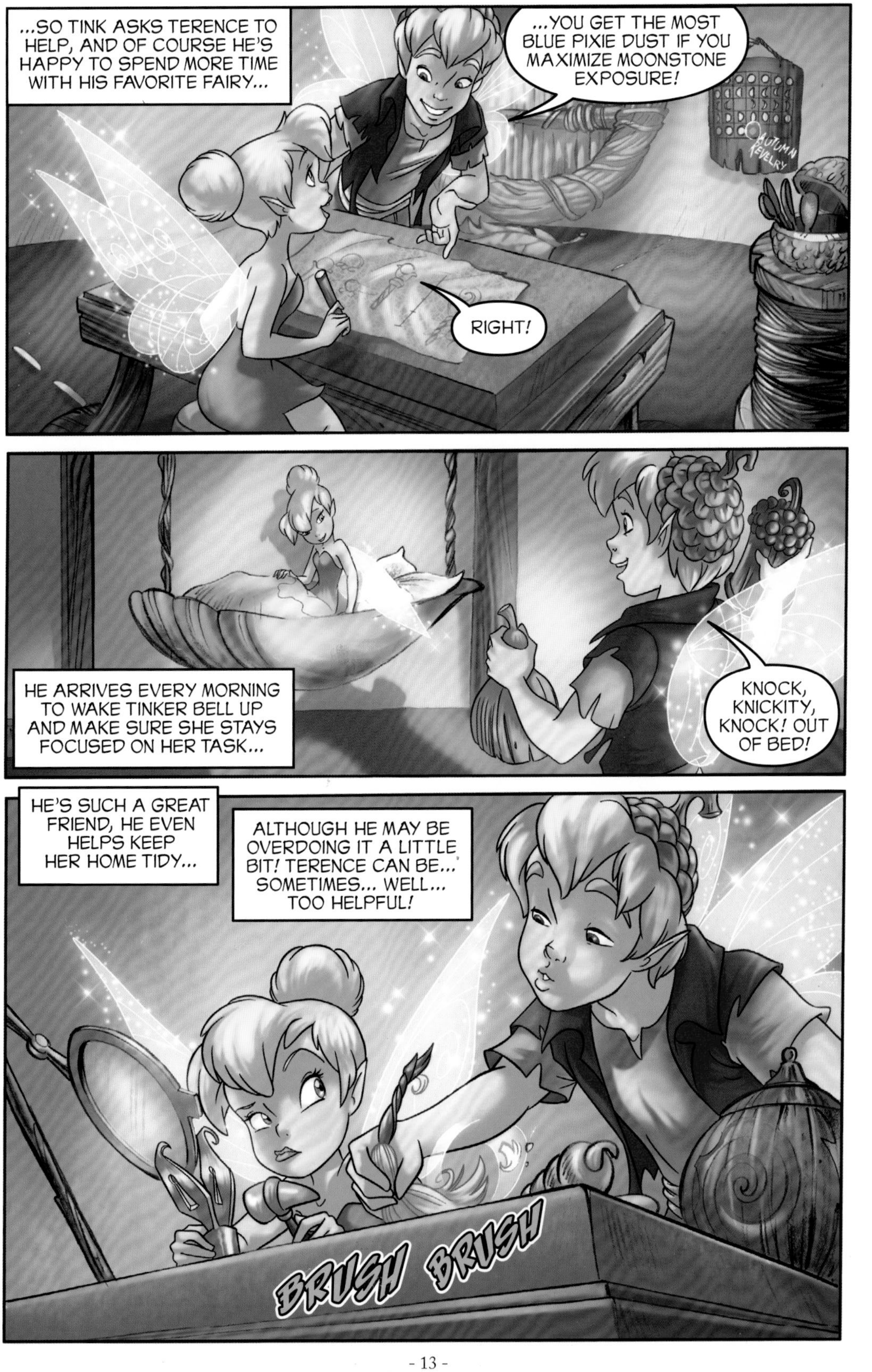
...SO TINK ASKS TERENCE TO HELP, AND OF COURSE HE'S HAPPY TO SPEND MORE TIME WITH HIS FAVORITE FAIRY...
...YOU GET THE MOST BLUE PIXIE DUST IF YOU MAXIMIZE MOONSTONE EXPOSURE!
AUTUMN REVELRY
RIGHT!
HE ARRIVES EVERY MORNING TO WAKE TINKER BELL UP AND MAKE SURE SHE STAYS FOCUSED ON HER TASK...
KNOCK, KNICKITY, KNOCK! OUT OF BED!
HE'S SUCH A GREAT FRIEND, HE EVEN HELPS KEEP HER HOME TIDY...
ALTHOUGH HE MAY BE OVERDOING IT A LITTLE BIT! TERENCE CAN BE... SOMETIMES... WELL... TOO HELPFUL!
BRUSH BRUSH

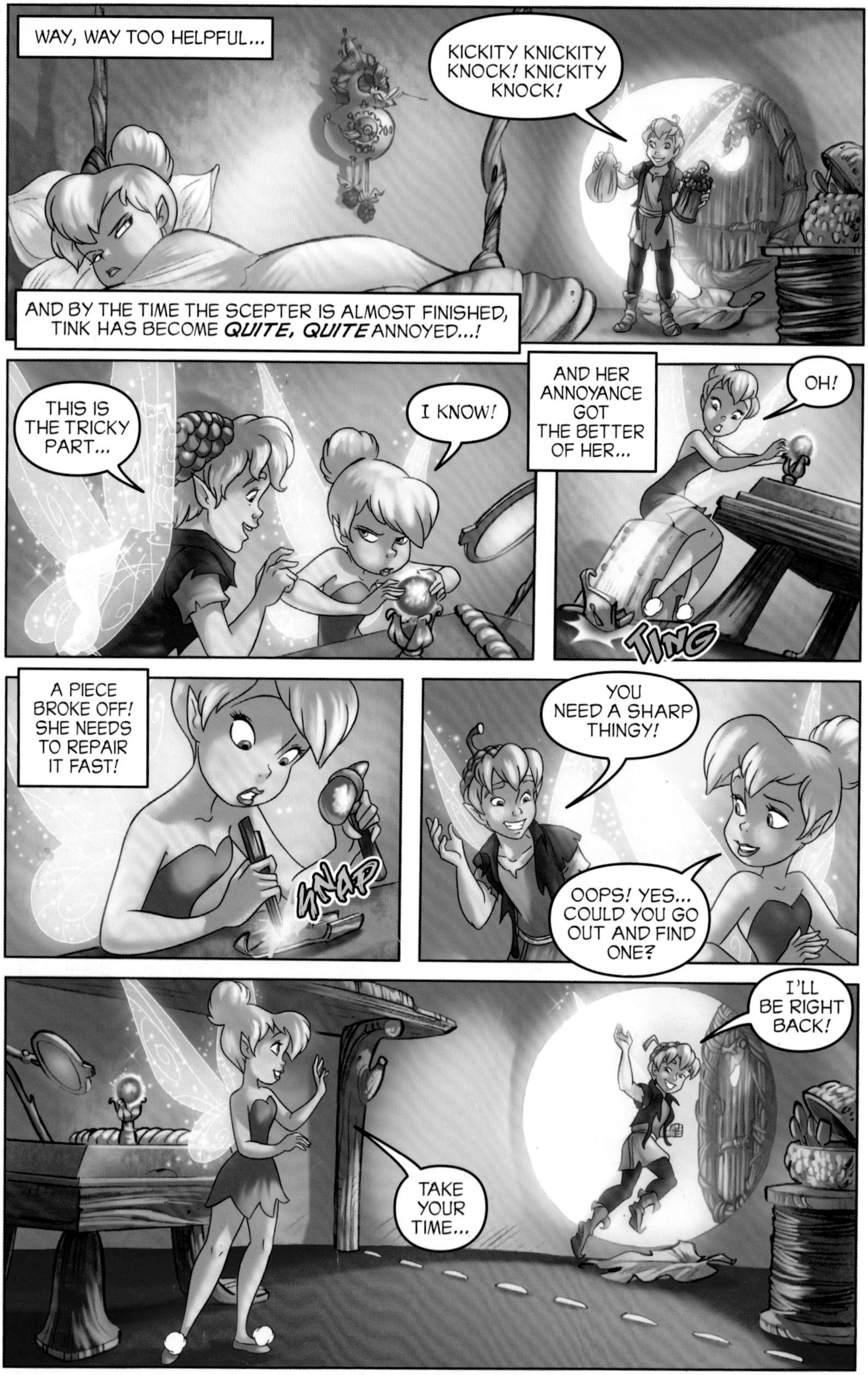
WAY, WAY TOO HELPFUL...
KICKITY KNICKITY KNOCK! KNICKITY KNOCK!
AND BY THE TIME THE SCEPTER IS ALMOST FINISHED, TINK HAS BECOME QUITE, QUITE ANNOYED...!
THIS IS THE TRICKY PART...
I KNOW!
AND HER ANNOYANCE GOT THE BETTER OF HER...
OH!
TING
A PIECE BROKE OFF! SHE NEEDS TO REPAIR IT FAST!
SNAP
YOU NEED A SHARP THINGY!
OOPS! YES... COULD YOU GO OUT AND FIND ONE?
I'LL BE RIGHT BACK!
TAKE YOUR TIME...

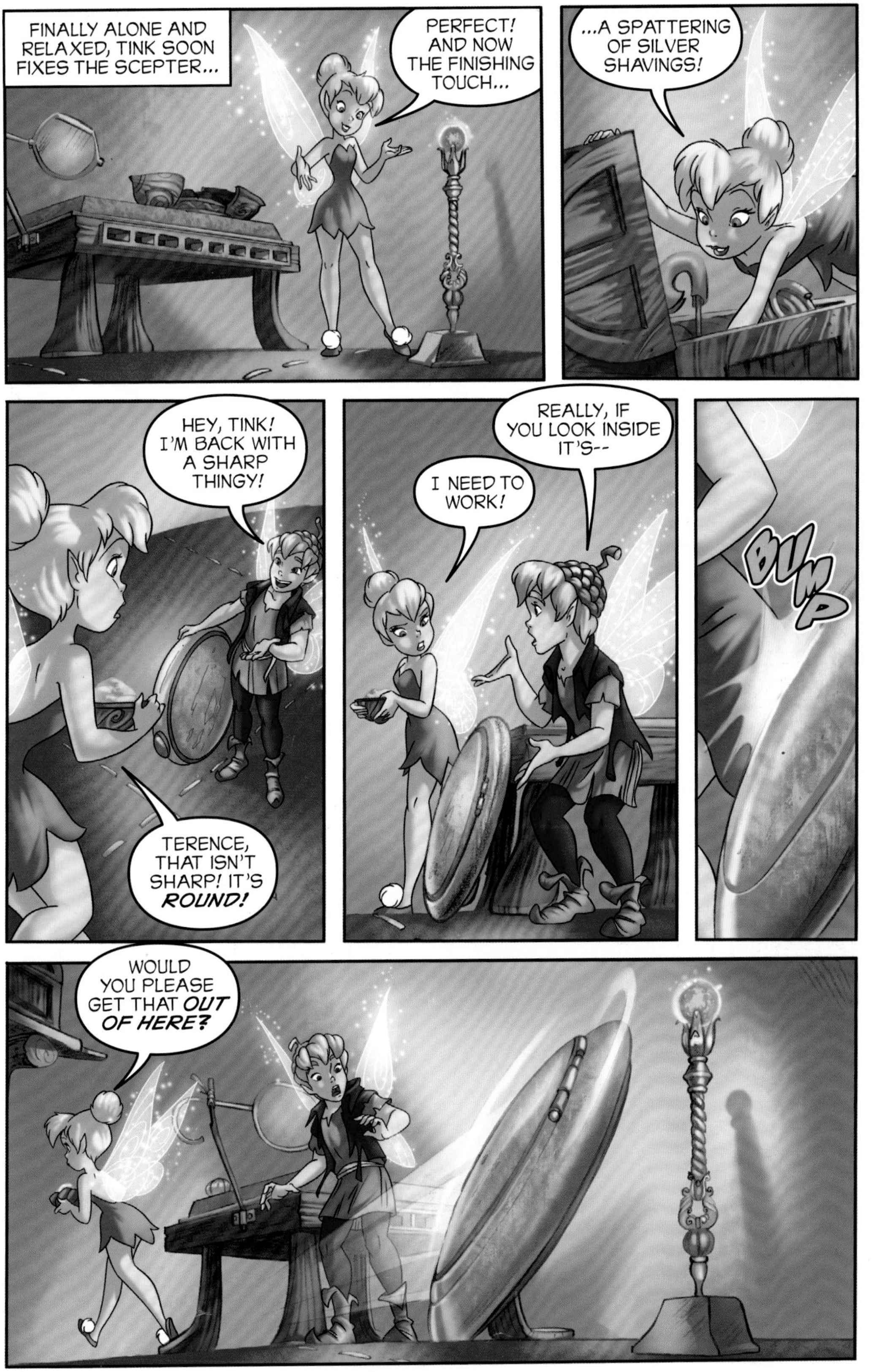
FINALLY ALONE AND RELAXED, TINK SOON FIXES THE SCEPTER...
PERFECT! AND NOW THE FINISHING TOUCH...
...A SPATTERING OF SILVER SHAVINGS!
HEY, TINK! I'M BACK WITH A SHARP THINGY!
TERENCE, THAT ISN'T SHARP! IT'S ROUND!
REALLY, IF YOU LOOK INSIDE IT'S--
I NEED TO WORK!
BUMP
WOULD YOU PLEASE GET THAT OUT OF HERE?

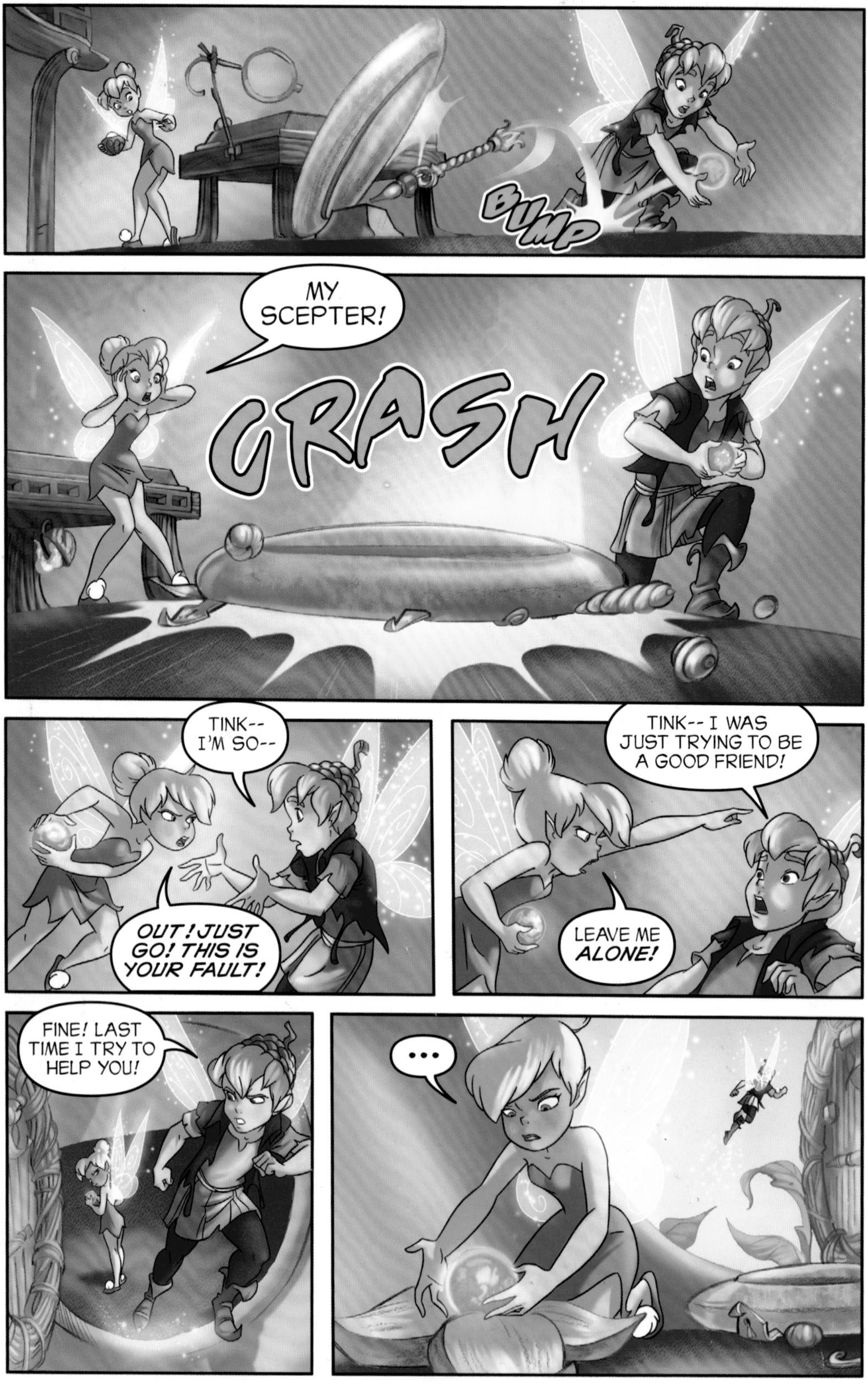

BUMP
MY SCEPTER!
CRASH
TINK-- I'M SO--
OUT! JUST GO! THIS IS YOUR FAULT!
TINK-- I WAS JUST TRYING TO BE A GOOD FRIEND!
LEAVE ME ALONE!
FINE! LAST TIME I TRY TO HELP YOU!
...

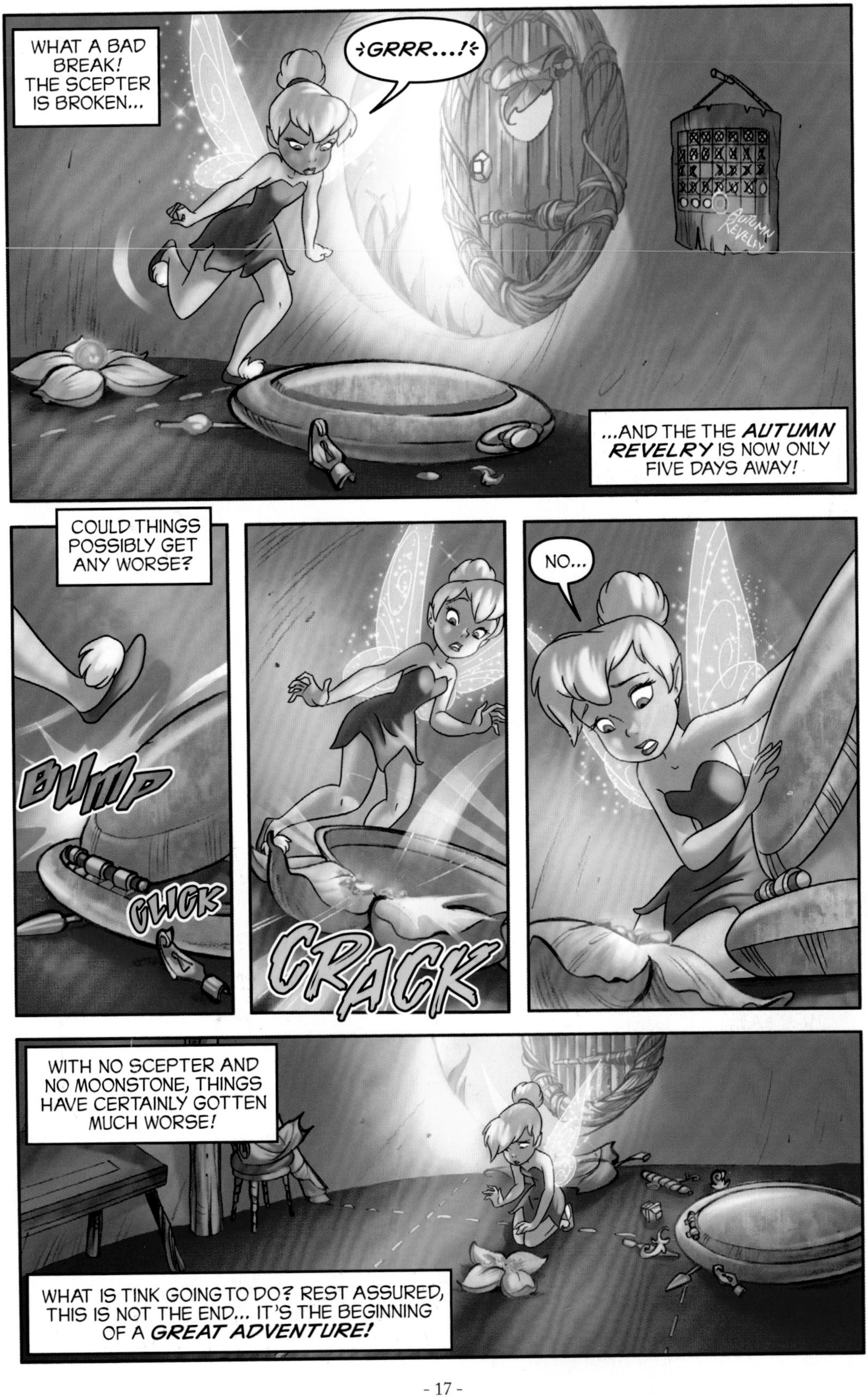

WHAT A BAD BREAK! THE SCEPTER IS BROKEN...
GRRR...!
AUTUMN REVELRY
...AND THE THE AUTUMN REVELRY IS NOW ONLY FIVE DAYS AWAY!
COULD THINGS POSSIBLY GET ANY WORSE?
BUMP
CLICK
CRACK
NO...
WITH NO SCEPTER AND NO MOONSTONE, THINGS HAVE CERTAINLY GOTTEN MUCH WORSE!
WHAT IS TINK GOING TO DO? REST ASSURED, THIS IS NOT THE END... IT'S THE BEGINNING OF A GREAT ADVENTURE!

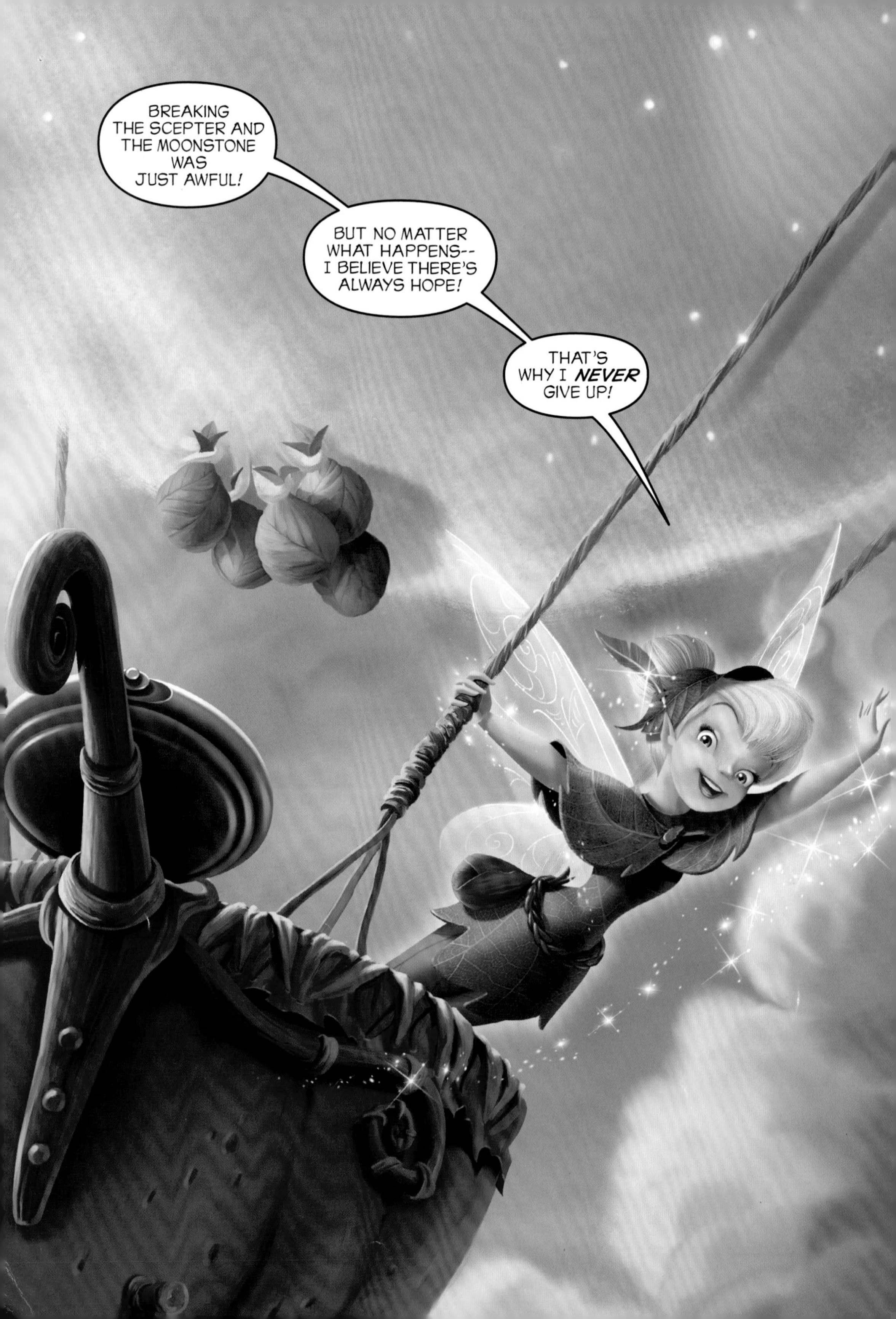
BREAKING THE SCEPTER AND THE MOONSTONE WAS JUST AWFUL!
BUT NO MATTER WHAT HAPPENS-- I BELIEVE THERE'S ALWAYS HOPE!
THAT'S WHY I ***NEVER*** GIVE UP!

TOWARDS THE ISLAND

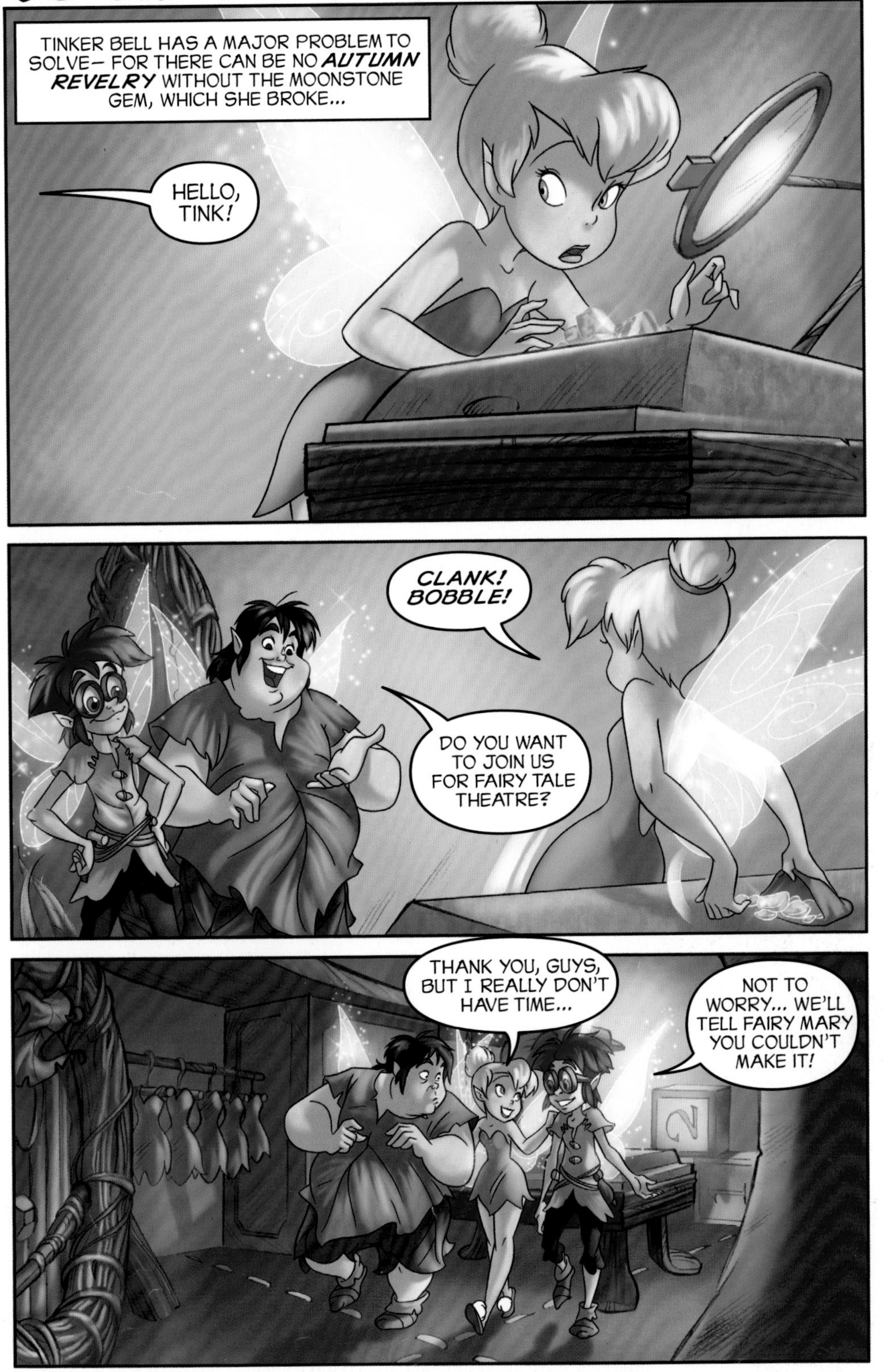
TINKER BELL HAS A MAJOR PROBLEM TO SOLVE– FOR THERE CAN BE NO *AUTUMN REVELRY* WITHOUT THE MOONSTONE GEM, WHICH SHE BROKE...
HELLO, TINK!
CLANK! BOBBLE!
DO YOU WANT TO JOIN US FOR FAIRY TALE THEATRE?
THANK YOU, GUYS, BUT I REALLY DON'T HAVE TIME...
NOT TO WORRY... WE'LL TELL FAIRY MARY YOU COULDN'T MAKE IT!

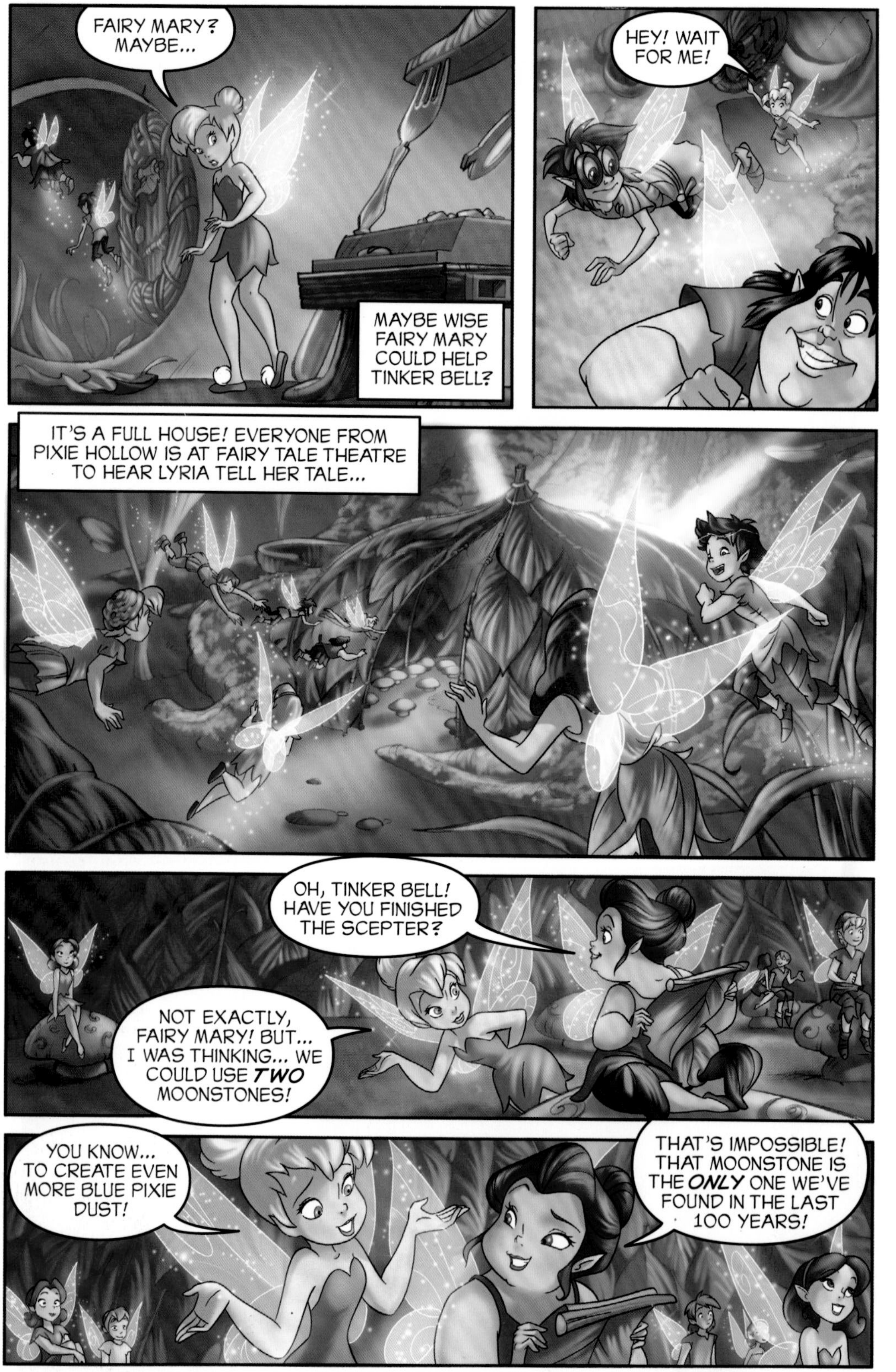
FAIRY MARY? MAYBE...
MAYBE WISE FAIRY MARY COULD HELP TINKER BELL?
HEY! WAIT FOR ME!
IT'S A FULL HOUSE! EVERYONE FROM PIXIE HOLLOW IS AT FAIRY TALE THEATRE TO HEAR LYRIA TELL HER TALE...
OH, TINKER BELL! HAVE YOU FINISHED THE SCEPTER?
NOT EXACTLY, FAIRY MARY! BUT... I WAS THINKING... WE COULD USE *TWO* MOONSTONES!
YOU KNOW... TO CREATE EVEN MORE BLUE PIXIE DUST!
THAT'S IMPOSSIBLE! THAT MOONSTONE IS THE *ONLY* ONE WE'VE FOUND IN THE LAST 100 YEARS!

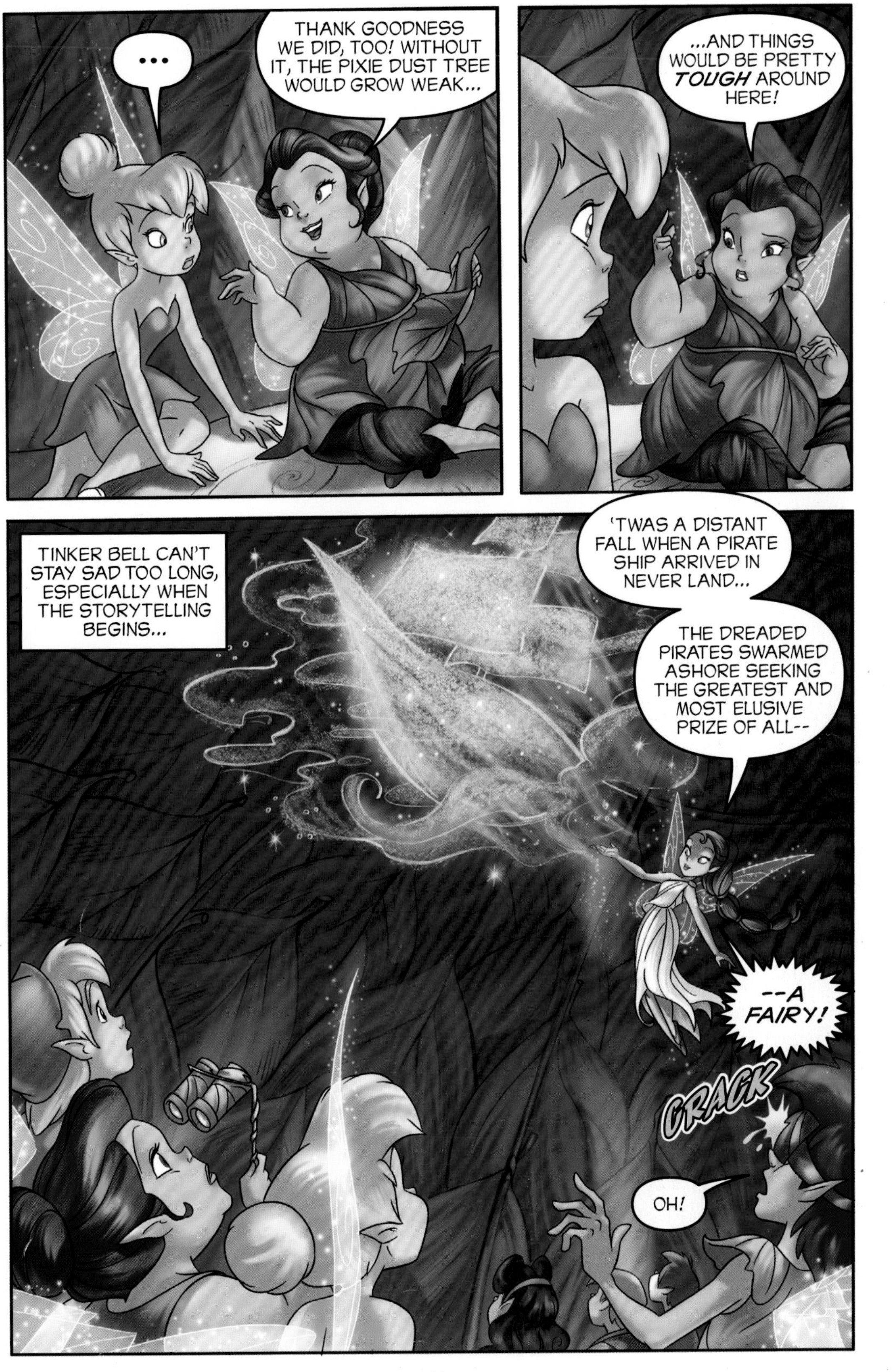
...
THANK GOODNESS WE DID, TOO! WITHOUT IT, THE PIXIE DUST TREE WOULD GROW WEAK...
...AND THINGS WOULD BE PRETTY TOUGH AROUND HERE!
TINKER BELL CAN'T STAY SAD TOO LONG, ESPECIALLY WHEN THE STORYTELLING BEGINS...
'TWAS A DISTANT FALL WHEN A PIRATE SHIP ARRIVED IN NEVER LAND...
THE DREADED PIRATES SWARMED ASHORE SEEKING THE GREATEST AND MOST ELUSIVE PRIZE OF ALL--
--A FAIRY!
CRACK
OH!

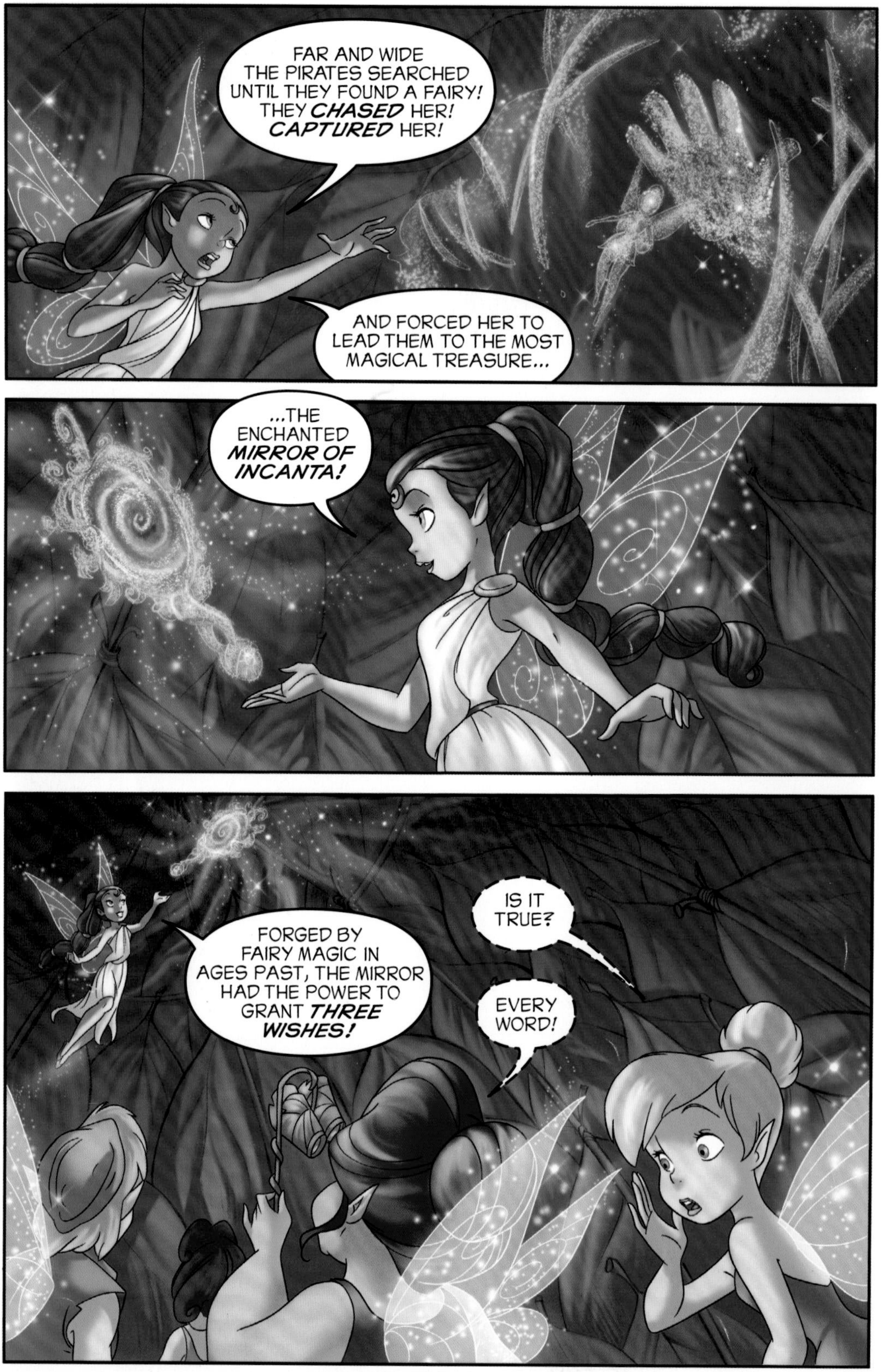
FAR AND WIDE THE PIRATES SEARCHED UNTIL THEY FOUND A FAIRY! THEY *CHASED* HER! *CAPTURED* HER!
AND FORCED HER TO LEAD THEM TO THE MOST MAGICAL TREASURE...
...THE ENCHANTED *MIRROR OF INCANTA!*
FORGED BY FAIRY MAGIC IN AGES PAST, THE MIRROR HAD THE POWER TO GRANT *THREE WISHES!*
IS IT TRUE?
EVERY WORD!

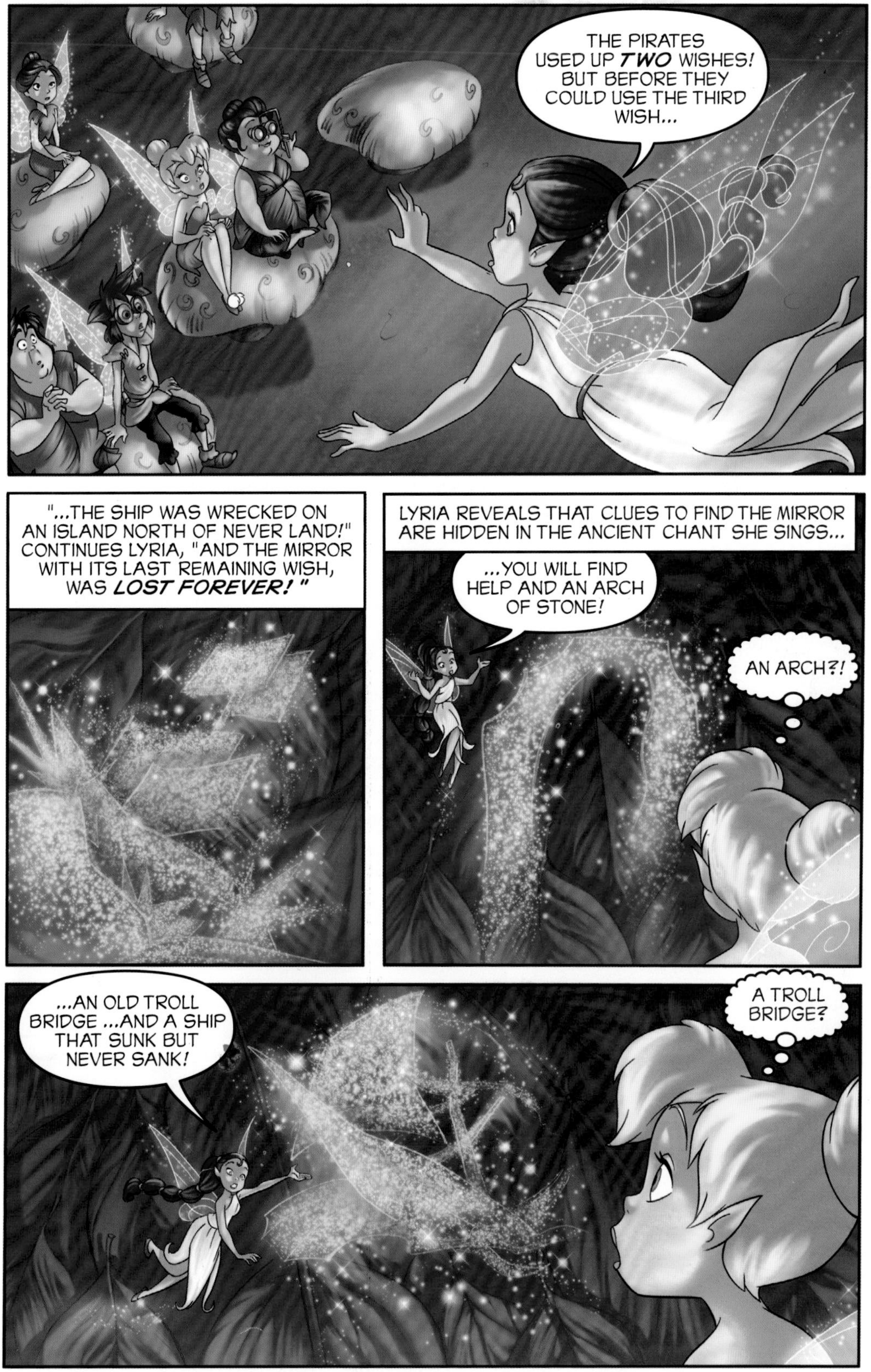
THE PIRATES USED UP TWO WISHES! BUT BEFORE THEY COULD USE THE THIRD WISH...
"...THE SHIP WAS WRECKED ON AN ISLAND NORTH OF NEVER LAND!" CONTINUES LYRIA, "AND THE MIRROR WITH ITS LAST REMAINING WISH, WAS LOST FOREVER!"
LYRIA REVEALS THAT CLUES TO FIND THE MIRROR ARE HIDDEN IN THE ANCIENT CHANT SHE SINGS...
...YOU WILL FIND HELP AND AN ARCH OF STONE!
AN ARCH?!
...AN OLD TROLL BRIDGE ...AND A SHIP THAT SUNK BUT NEVER SANK!
A TROLL BRIDGE?

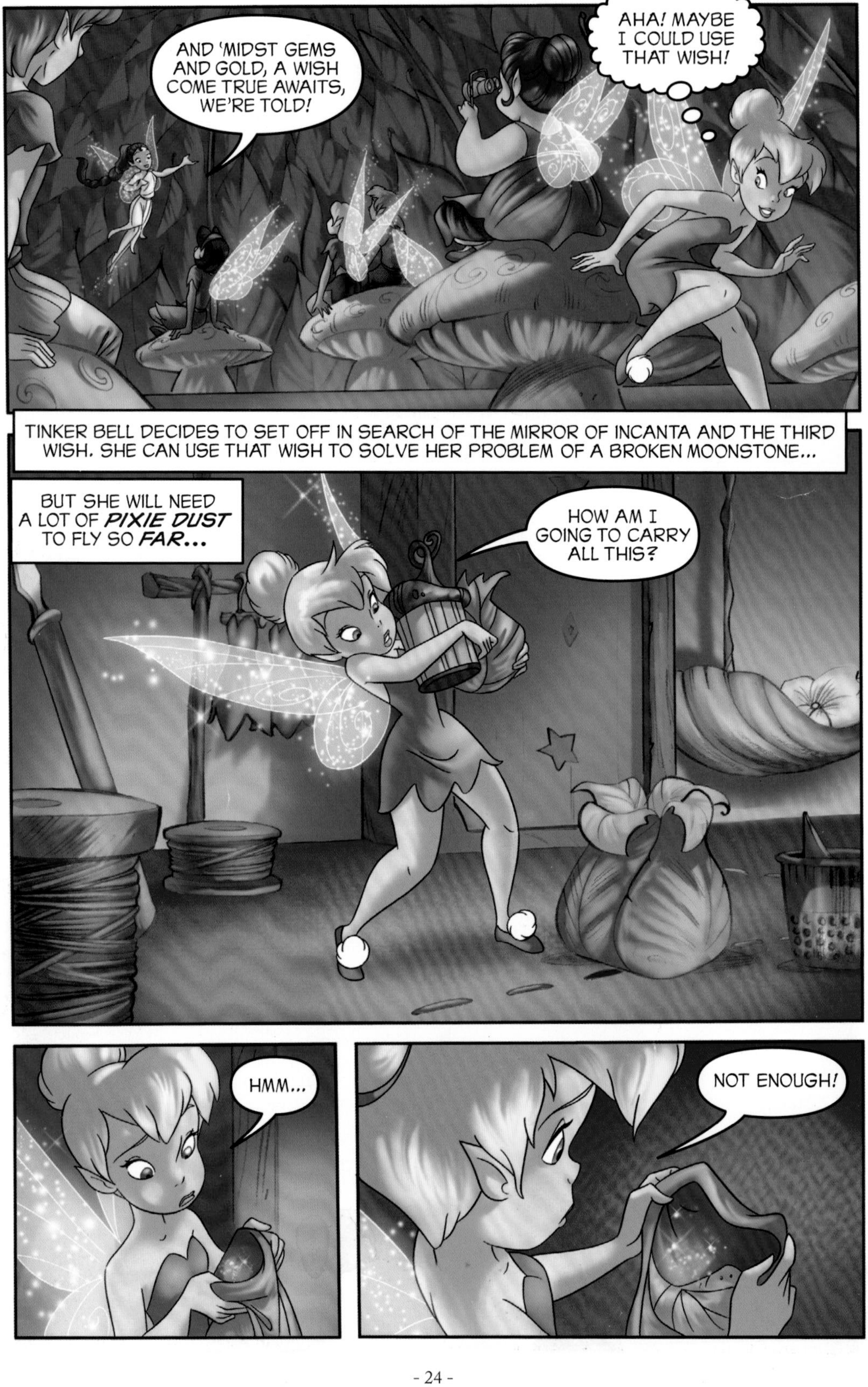
AND 'MIDST GEMS AND GOLD, A WISH COME TRUE AWAITS, WE'RE TOLD!
AHA! MAYBE I COULD USE THAT WISH!
TINKER BELL DECIDES TO SET OFF IN SEARCH OF THE MIRROR OF INCANTA AND THE THIRD WISH. SHE CAN USE THAT WISH TO SOLVE HER PROBLEM OF A BROKEN MOONSTONE...
BUT SHE WILL NEED A LOT OF *PIXIE DUST* TO FLY SO *FAR*...
HOW AM I GOING TO CARRY ALL THIS?
HMM...
NOT ENOUGH!

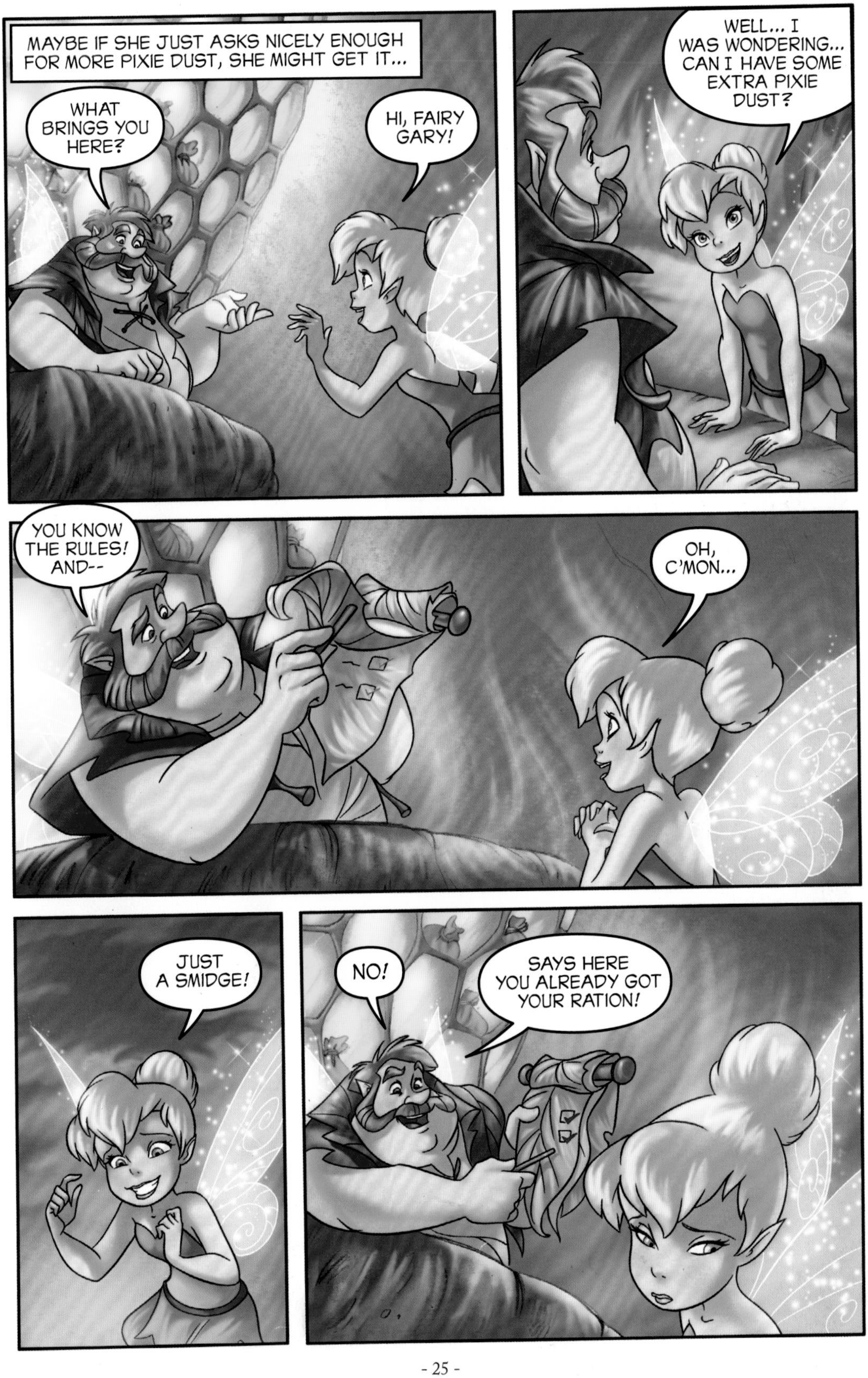
MAYBE IF SHE JUST ASKS NICELY ENOUGH FOR MORE PIXIE DUST, SHE MIGHT GET IT...
HI, FAIRY GARY!
WHAT BRINGS YOU HERE?
WELL... I WAS WONDERING... CAN I HAVE SOME EXTRA PIXIE DUST?
YOU KNOW THE RULES! AND--
OH, C'MON...
JUST A SMIDGE!
NO!
SAYS HERE YOU ALREADY GOT YOUR RATION!

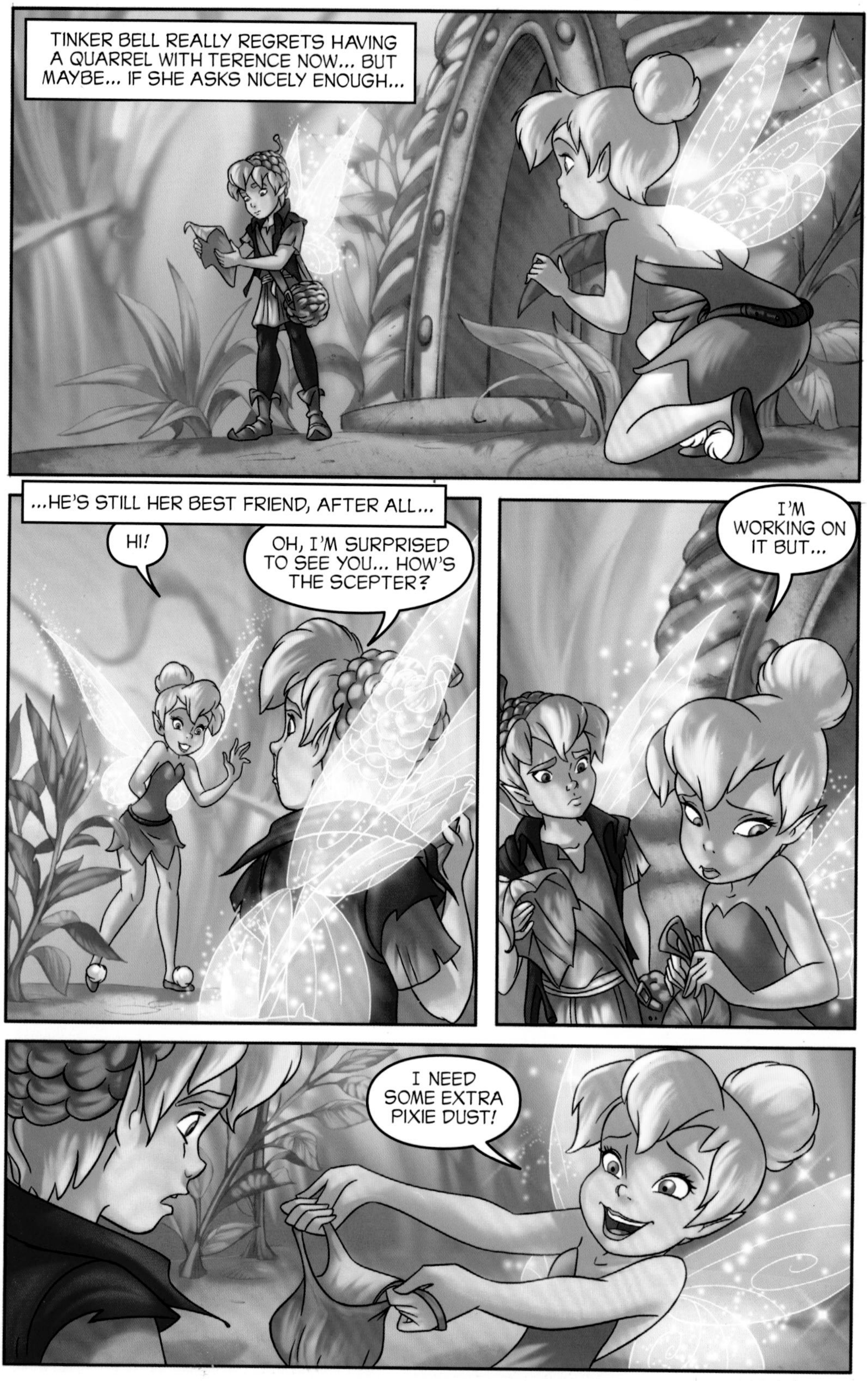
TINKER BELL REALLY REGRETS HAVING A QUARREL WITH TERENCE NOW... BUT MAYBE... IF SHE ASKS NICELY ENOUGH...
...HE'S STILL HER BEST FRIEND, AFTER ALL...
HI!
OH, I'M SURPRISED TO SEE YOU... HOW'S THE SCEPTER?
I'M WORKING ON IT BUT...
I NEED SOME EXTRA PIXIE DUST!

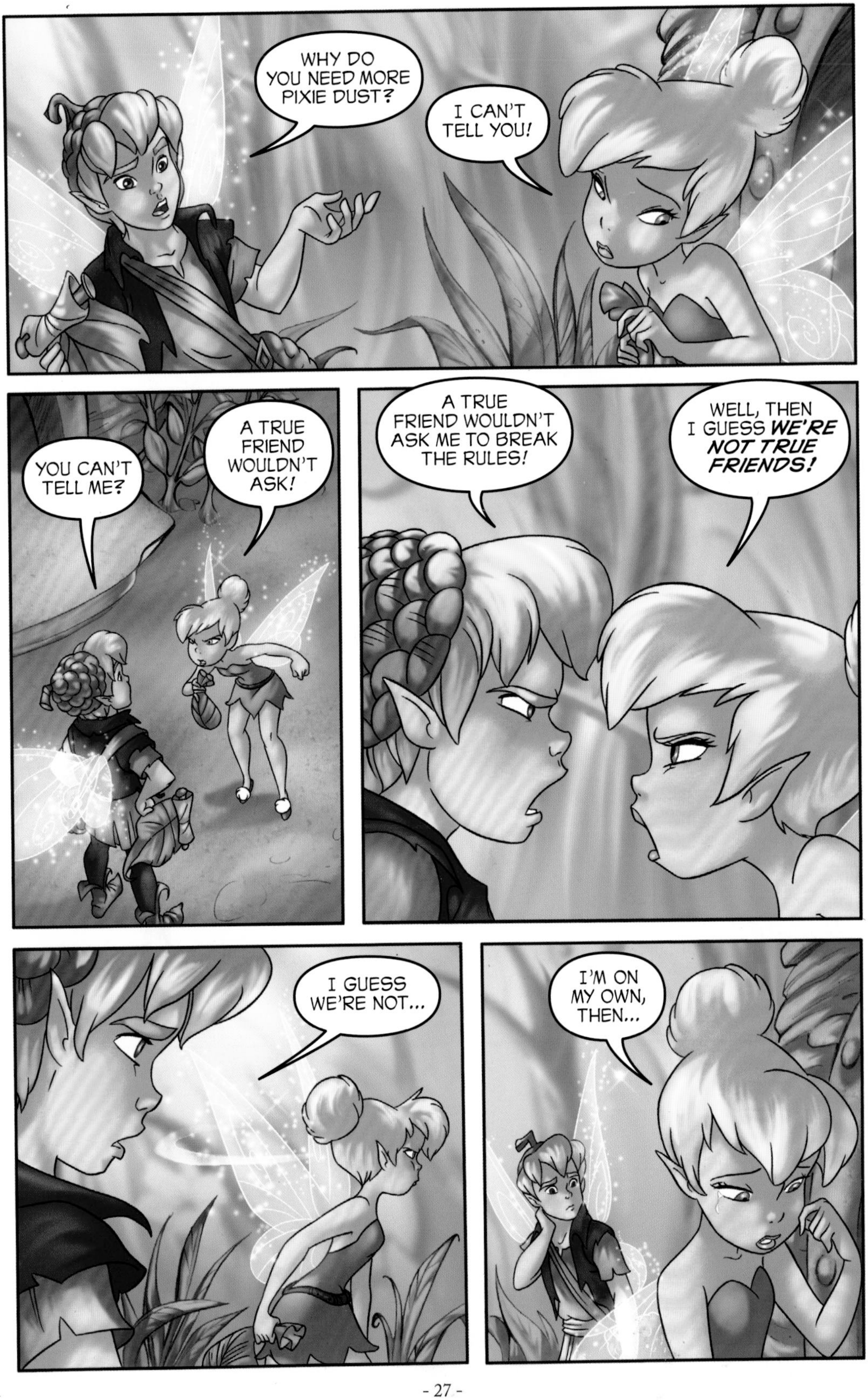

WHY DO YOU NEED MORE PIXIE DUST?
I CAN'T TELL YOU!
YOU CAN'T TELL ME?
A TRUE FRIEND WOULDN'T ASK!
A TRUE FRIEND WOULDN'T ASK ME TO BREAK THE RULES!
WELL, THEN I GUESS *WE'RE NOT TRUE FRIENDS!*
I GUESS WE'RE NOT...
I'M ON MY OWN, THEN...

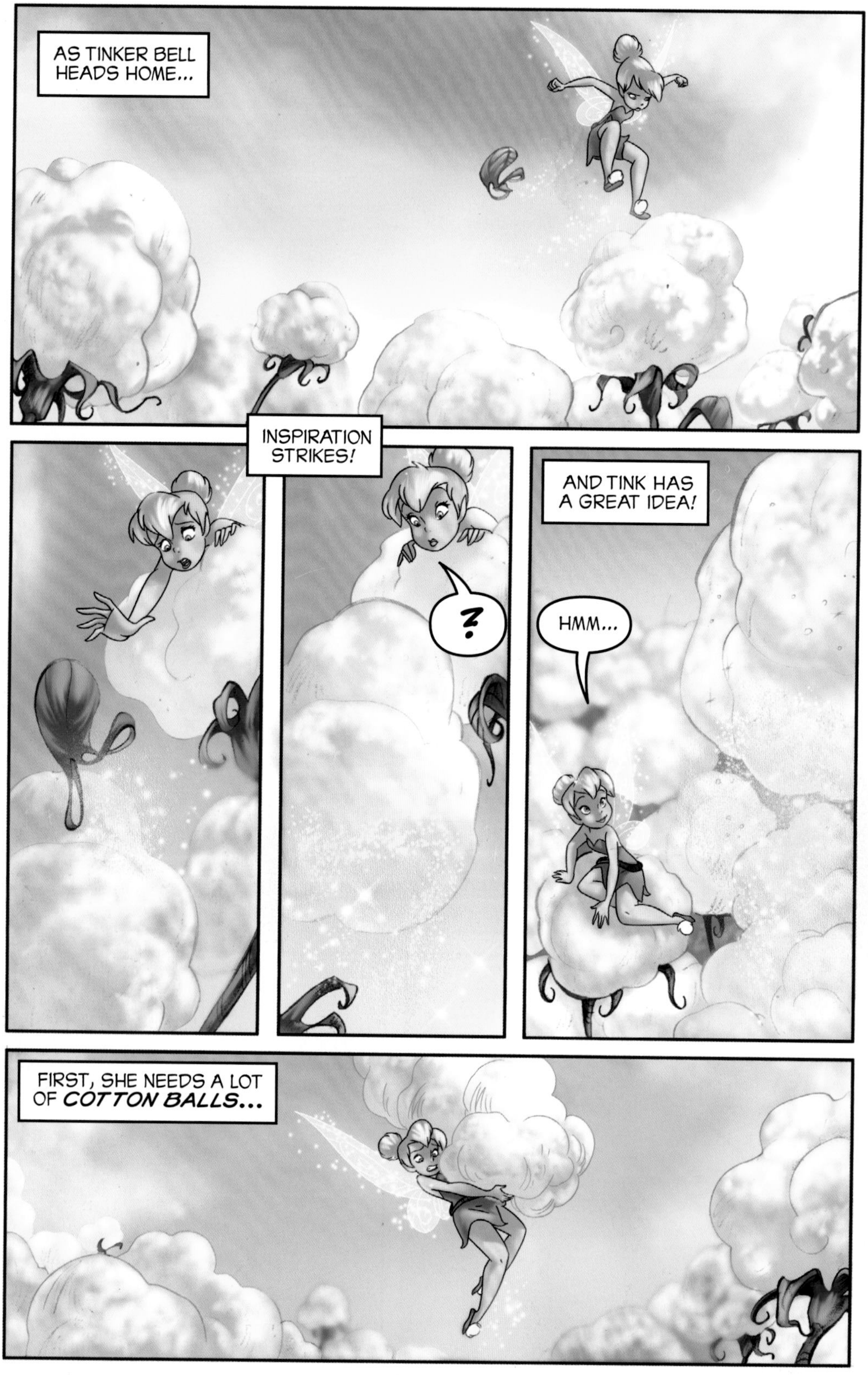
AS TINKER BELL HEADS HOME...
INSPIRATION STRIKES!
?
AND TINK HAS A GREAT IDEA!
HMM...
FIRST, SHE NEEDS A LOT OF COTTON BALLS...

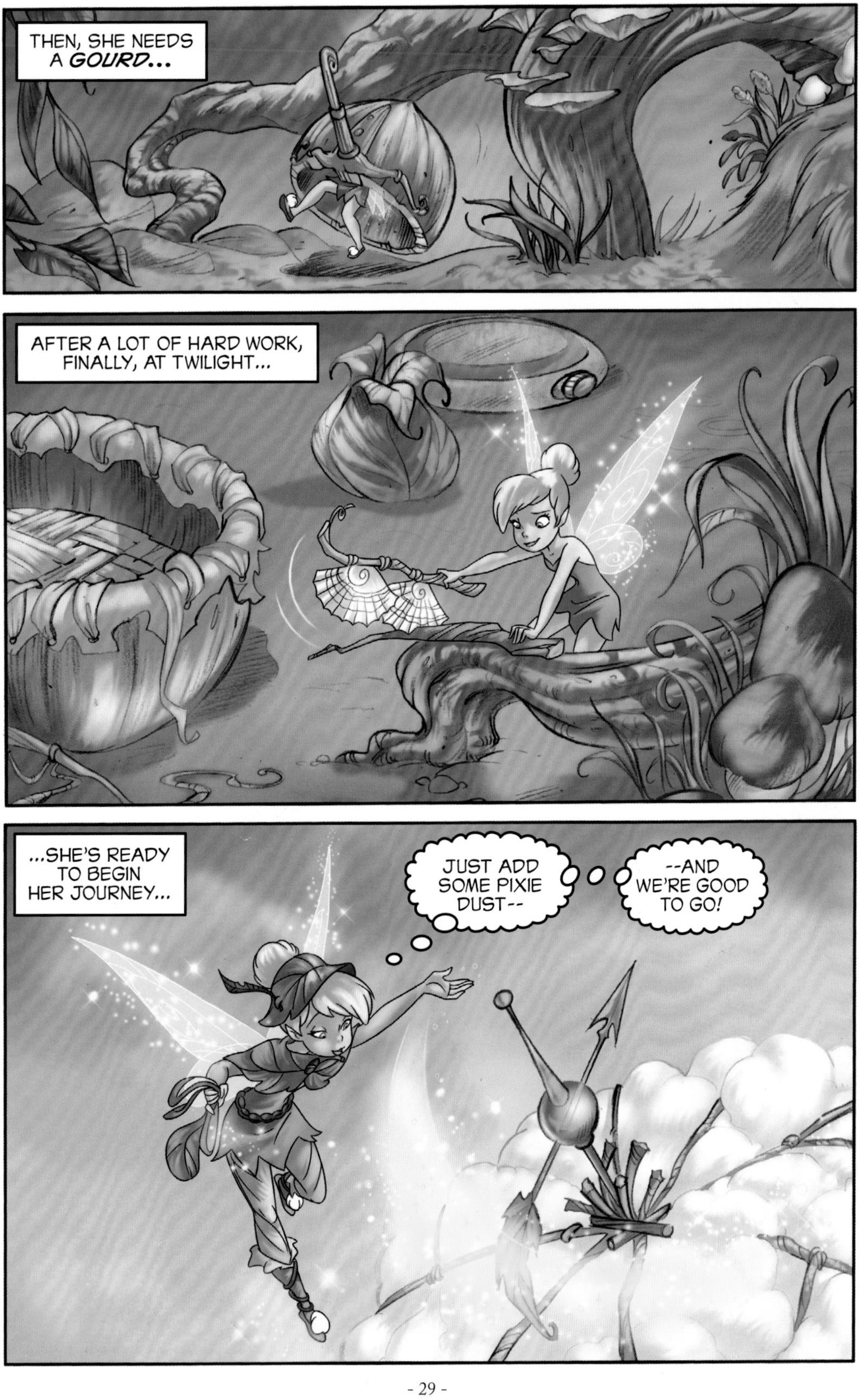
THEN, SHE NEEDS A GOURD...
AFTER A LOT OF HARD WORK, FINALLY, AT TWILIGHT...
...SHE'S READY TO BEGIN HER JOURNEY...
JUST ADD SOME PIXIE DUST--
--AND WE'RE GOOD TO GO!

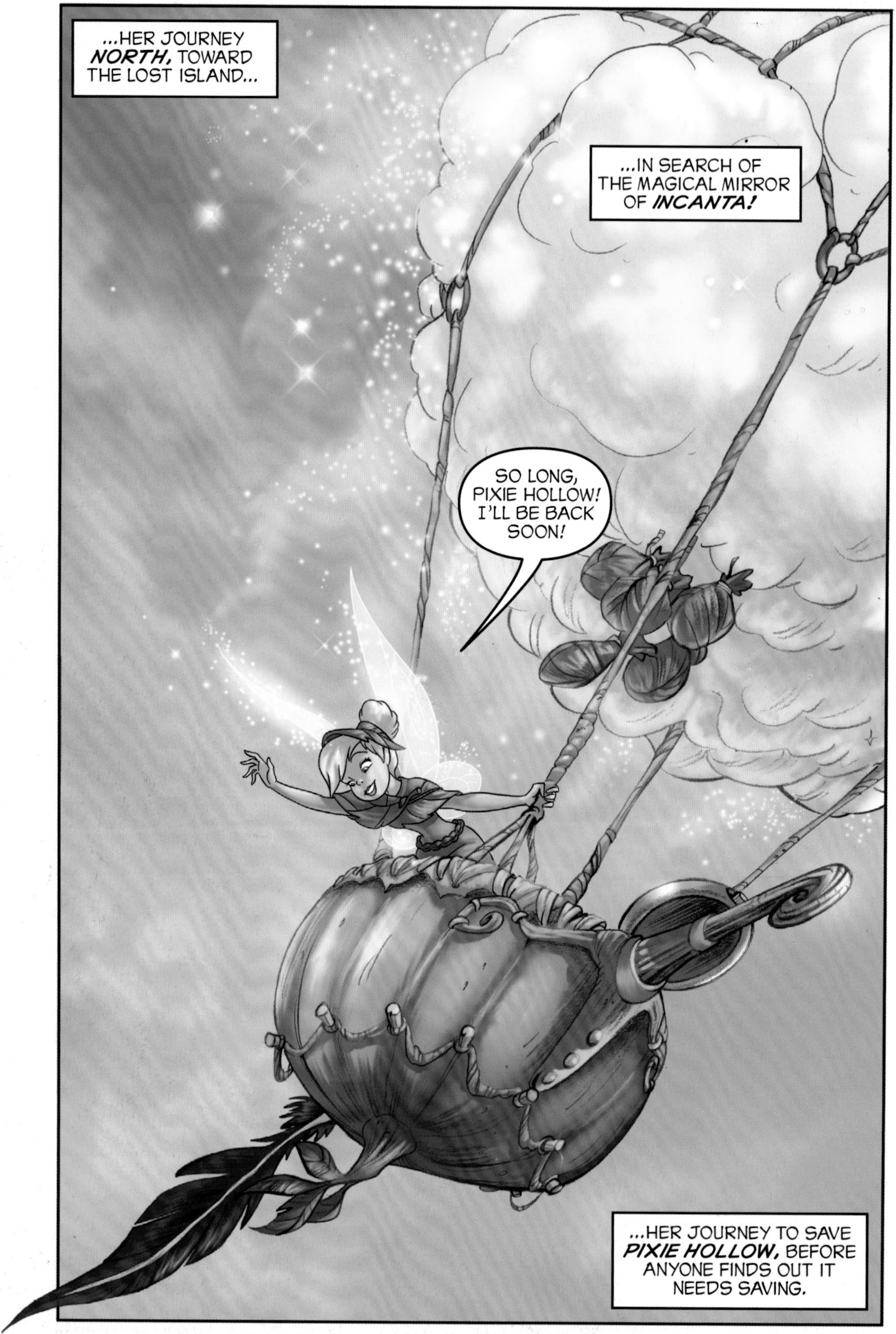
...HER JOURNEY NORTH, TOWARD THE LOST ISLAND...
...IN SEARCH OF THE MAGICAL MIRROR OF INCANTA!
SO LONG, PIXIE HOLLOW! I'LL BE BACK SOON!
...HER JOURNEY TO SAVE PIXIE HOLLOW, BEFORE ANYONE FINDS OUT IT NEEDS SAVING.

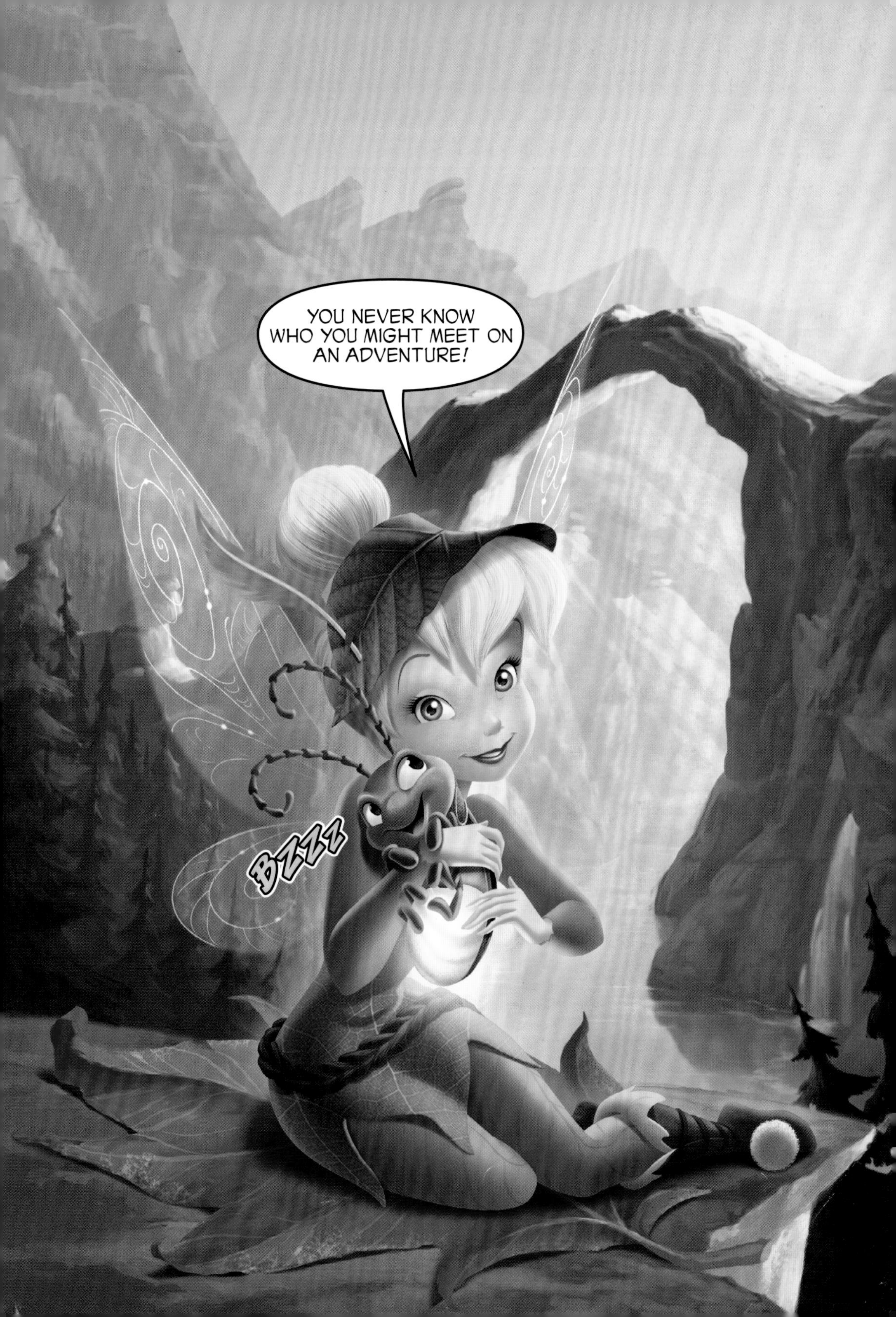
YOU NEVER KNOW WHO YOU MIGHT MEET ON AN ADVENTURE!
BZZZ

THE MAGICAL MIRROR OF INCANTA

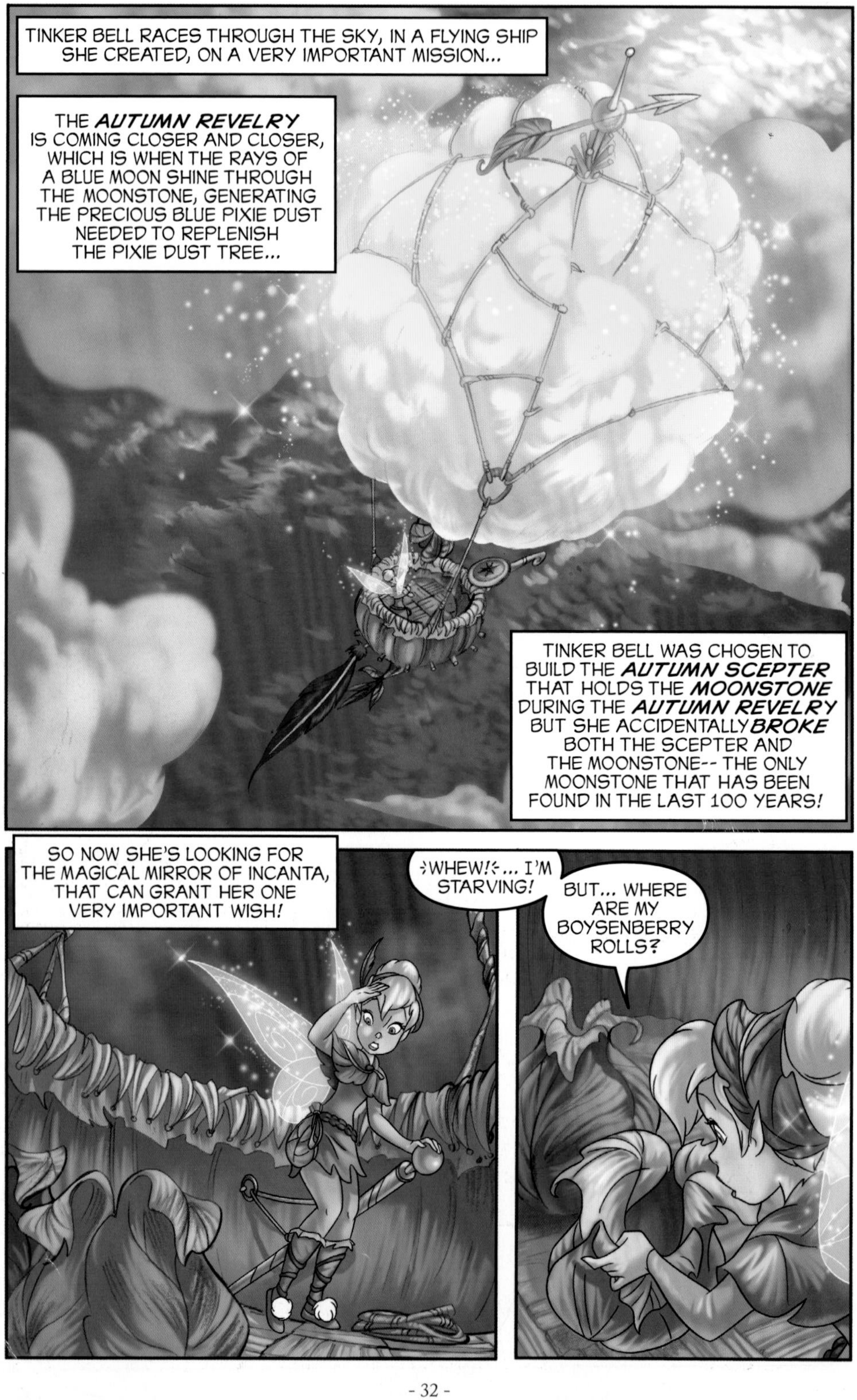

TINKER BELL RACES THROUGH THE SKY, IN A FLYING SHIP SHE CREATED, ON A VERY IMPORTANT MISSION...
THE *AUTUMN REVELRY* IS COMING CLOSER AND CLOSER, WHICH IS WHEN THE RAYS OF A BLUE MOON SHINE THROUGH THE MOONSTONE, GENERATING THE PRECIOUS BLUE PIXIE DUST NEEDED TO REPLENISH THE PIXIE DUST TREE...
TINKER BELL WAS CHOSEN TO BUILD THE *AUTUMN SCEPTER* THAT HOLDS THE *MOONSTONE* DURING THE *AUTUMN REVELRY* BUT SHE ACCIDENTALLY *BROKE* BOTH THE SCEPTER AND THE MOONSTONE-- THE ONLY MOONSTONE THAT HAS BEEN FOUND IN THE LAST 100 YEARS!
SO NOW SHE'S LOOKING FOR THE MAGICAL MIRROR OF INCANTA, THAT CAN GRANT HER ONE VERY IMPORTANT WISH!
WHEW!... I'M STARVING!
BUT... WHERE ARE MY BOYSENBERRY ROLLS?

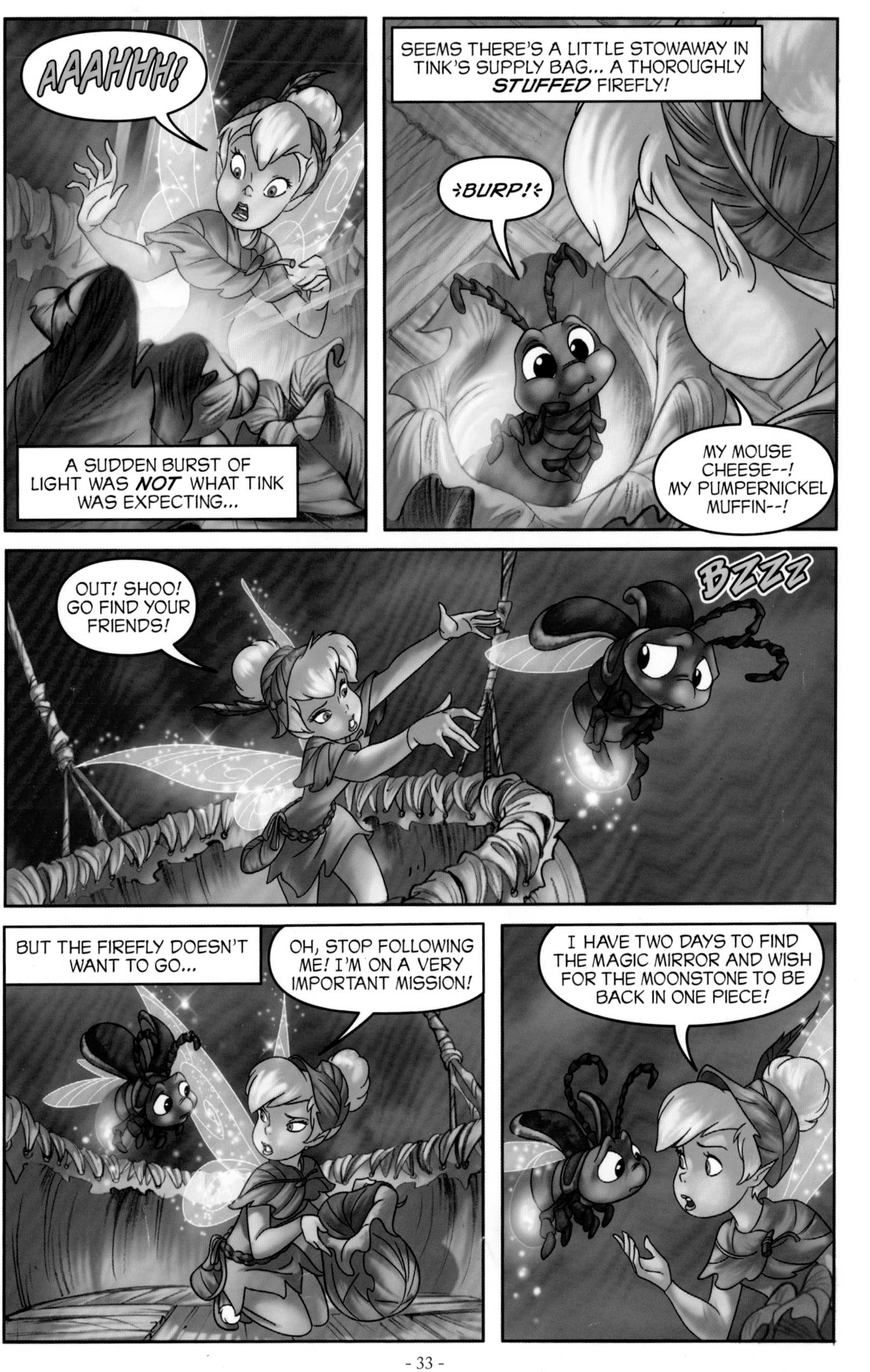
AAAHHH!
A SUDDEN BURST OF LIGHT WAS NOT WHAT TINK WAS EXPECTING...
SEEMS THERE'S A LITTLE STOWAWAY IN TINK'S SUPPLY BAG... A THOROUGHLY STUFFED FIREFLY!
BURP!
MY MOUSE CHEESE--! MY PUMPERNICKEL MUFFIN--!
OUT! SHOO! GO FIND YOUR FRIENDS!
BZZZ
BUT THE FIREFLY DOESN'T WANT TO GO...
OH, STOP FOLLOWING ME! I'M ON A VERY IMPORTANT MISSION!
I HAVE TWO DAYS TO FIND THE MAGIC MIRROR AND WISH FOR THE MOONSTONE TO BE BACK IN ONE PIECE!

IN THE DARKNESS, TINKER BELL HAS TROUBLE READING HER MAP UNTIL...

OH, ALRIGHT! YOU CAN STAY... FOR NOW! JUST DO ME A FAVOR...

BZZ

BZZ

HMM...

...IF YOU CAN *STAY RIGHT HERE!*

IF MY BEARINGS ARE ACCURATE, WE SHOULD SEE LAND SOON!

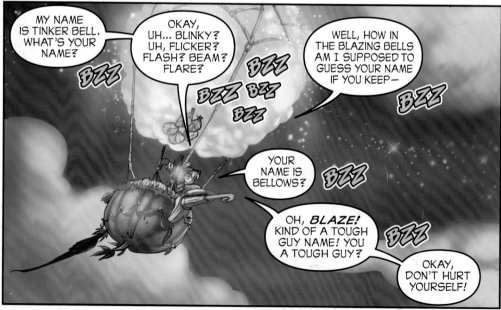

MY NAME IS TINKER BELL. WHAT'S YOUR NAME?

OKAY, UH... BLINKY? UH, FLICKER? FLASH? BEAM? FLARE?

WELL, HOW IN THE BLAZING BELLS AM I SUPPOSED TO GUESS YOUR NAME IF YOU KEEP—

BZZ

BZZ BZZ BZZ BZZ

BZZ

YOUR NAME IS BELLOWS?

BZZ

OH, *BLAZE!* KIND OF A TOUGH GUY NAME! YOU A TOUGH GUY?

BZZ

OKAY, DON'T HURT YOURSELF!

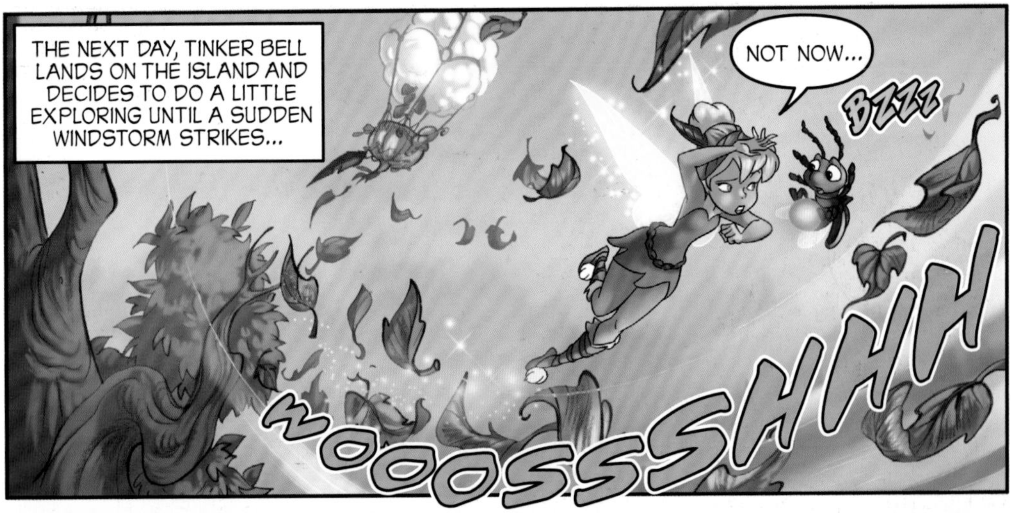
THE NEXT DAY, TINKER BELL LANDS ON THE ISLAND AND DECIDES TO DO A LITTLE EXPLORING UNTIL A SUDDEN WINDSTORM STRIKES...
NOT NOW...
BZZZ
WOOOSSSHHHH

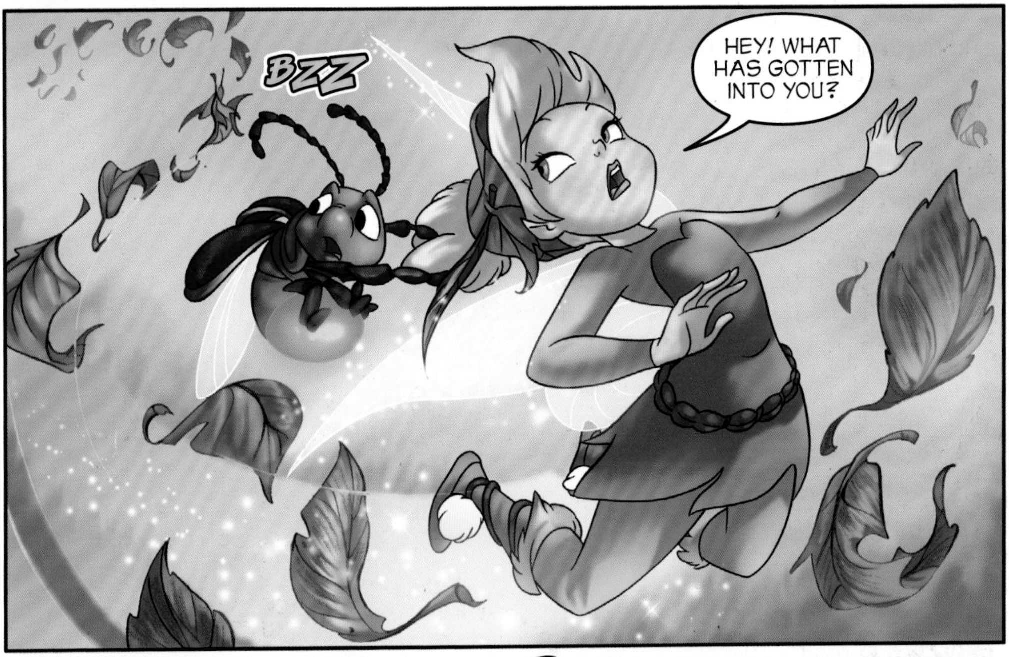
BZZ
HEY! WHAT HAS GOTTEN INTO YOU?

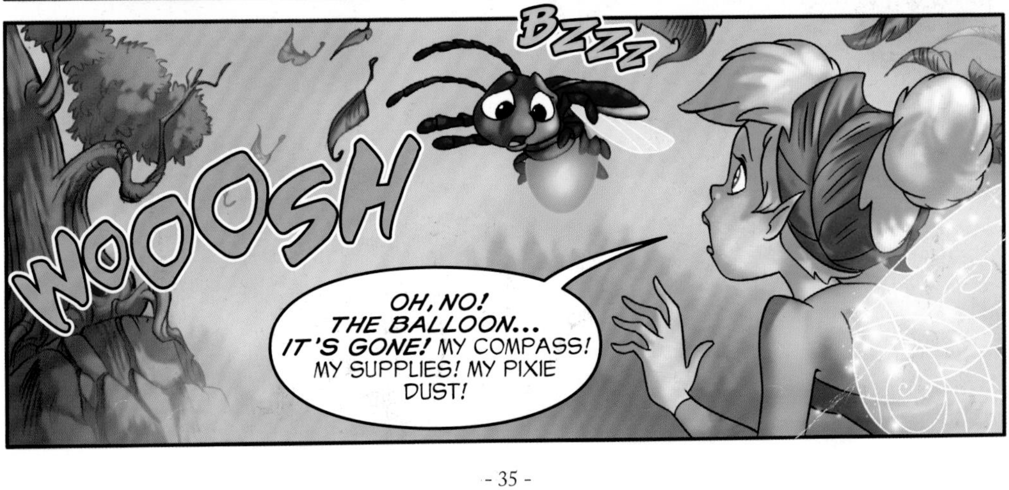
BZZZ
WOOOSH
OH, NO! THE BALLOON... IT'S GONE! MY COMPASS! MY SUPPLIES! MY PIXIE DUST!

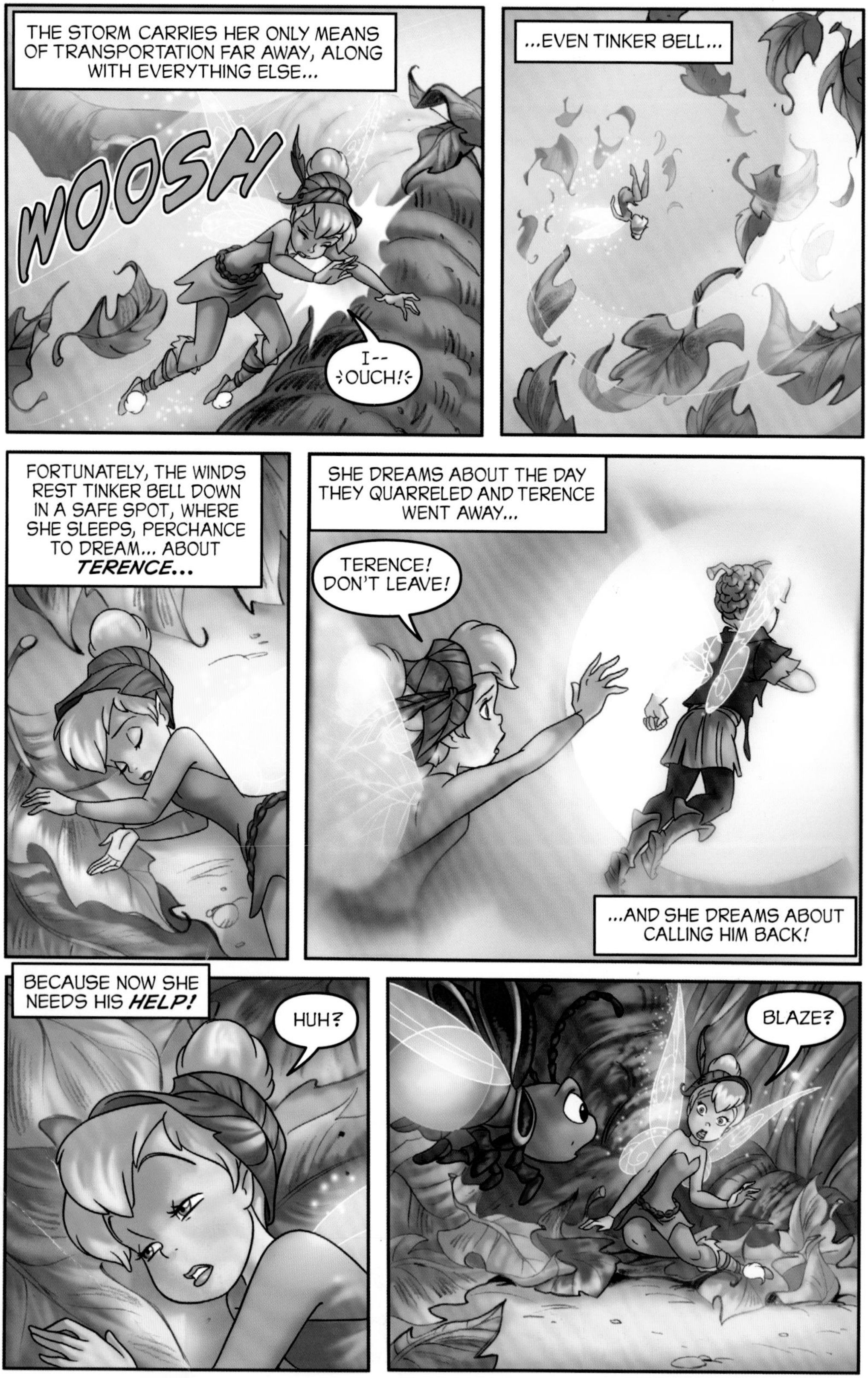

THE STORM CARRIES HER ONLY MEANS OF TRANSPORTATION FAR AWAY, ALONG WITH EVERYTHING ELSE...
WOOSH
I-- OUCH!
...EVEN TINKER BELL...
FORTUNATELY, THE WINDS REST TINKER BELL DOWN IN A SAFE SPOT, WHERE SHE SLEEPS, PERCHANCE TO DREAM... ABOUT *TERENCE...*
SHE DREAMS ABOUT THE DAY THEY QUARRELED AND TERENCE WENT AWAY...
TERENCE! DON'T LEAVE!
...AND SHE DREAMS ABOUT CALLING HIM BACK!
BECAUSE NOW SHE NEEDS HIS *HELP!*
HUH?
BLAZE?

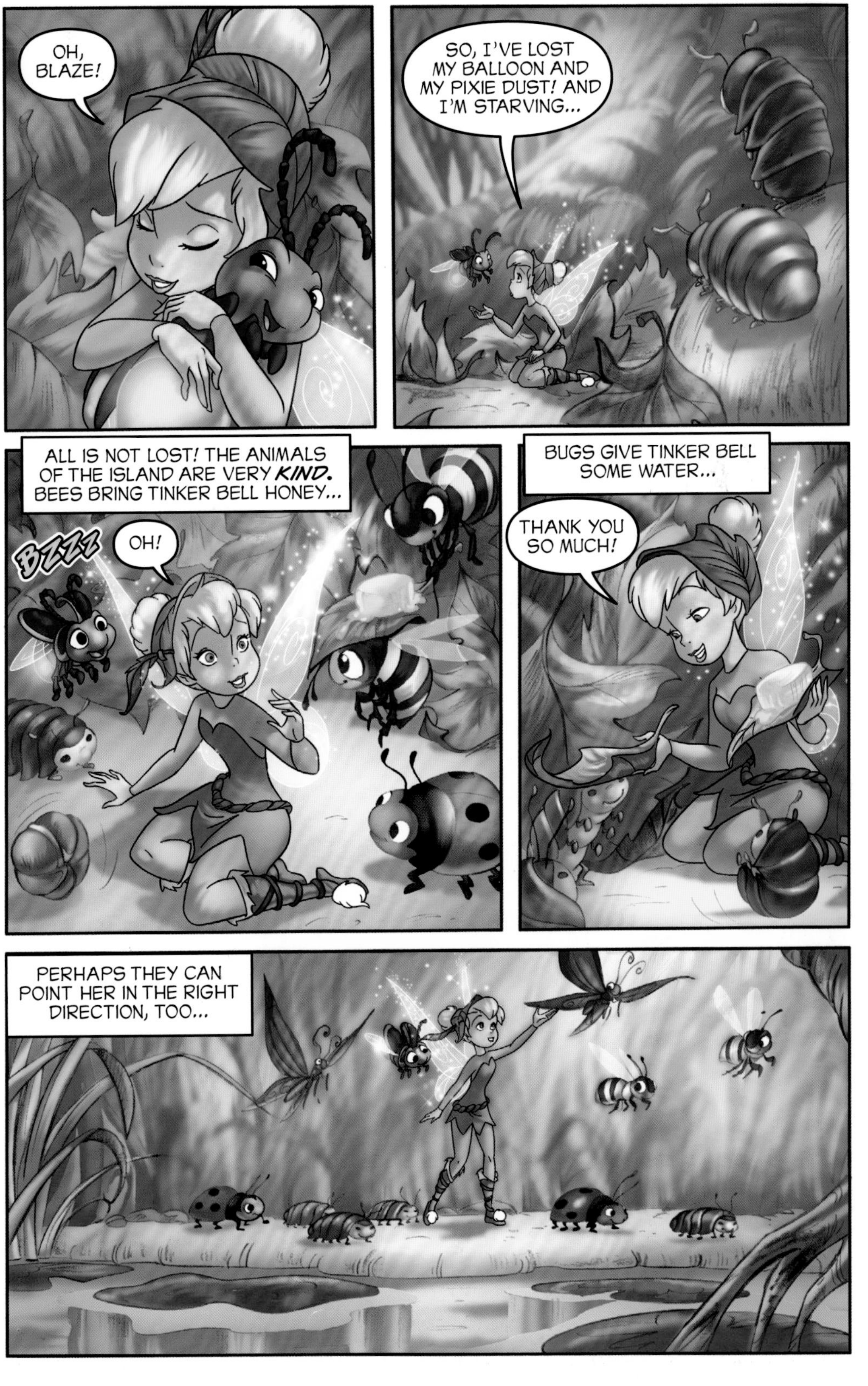

OH, BLAZE!
SO, I'VE LOST MY BALLOON AND MY PIXIE DUST! AND I'M STARVING...
ALL IS NOT LOST! THE ANIMALS OF THE ISLAND ARE VERY KIND. BEES BRING TINKER BELL HONEY...
BZZZ
OH!
BUGS GIVE TINKER BELL SOME WATER...
THANK YOU SO MUCH!
PERHAPS THEY CAN POINT HER IN THE RIGHT DIRECTION, TOO...

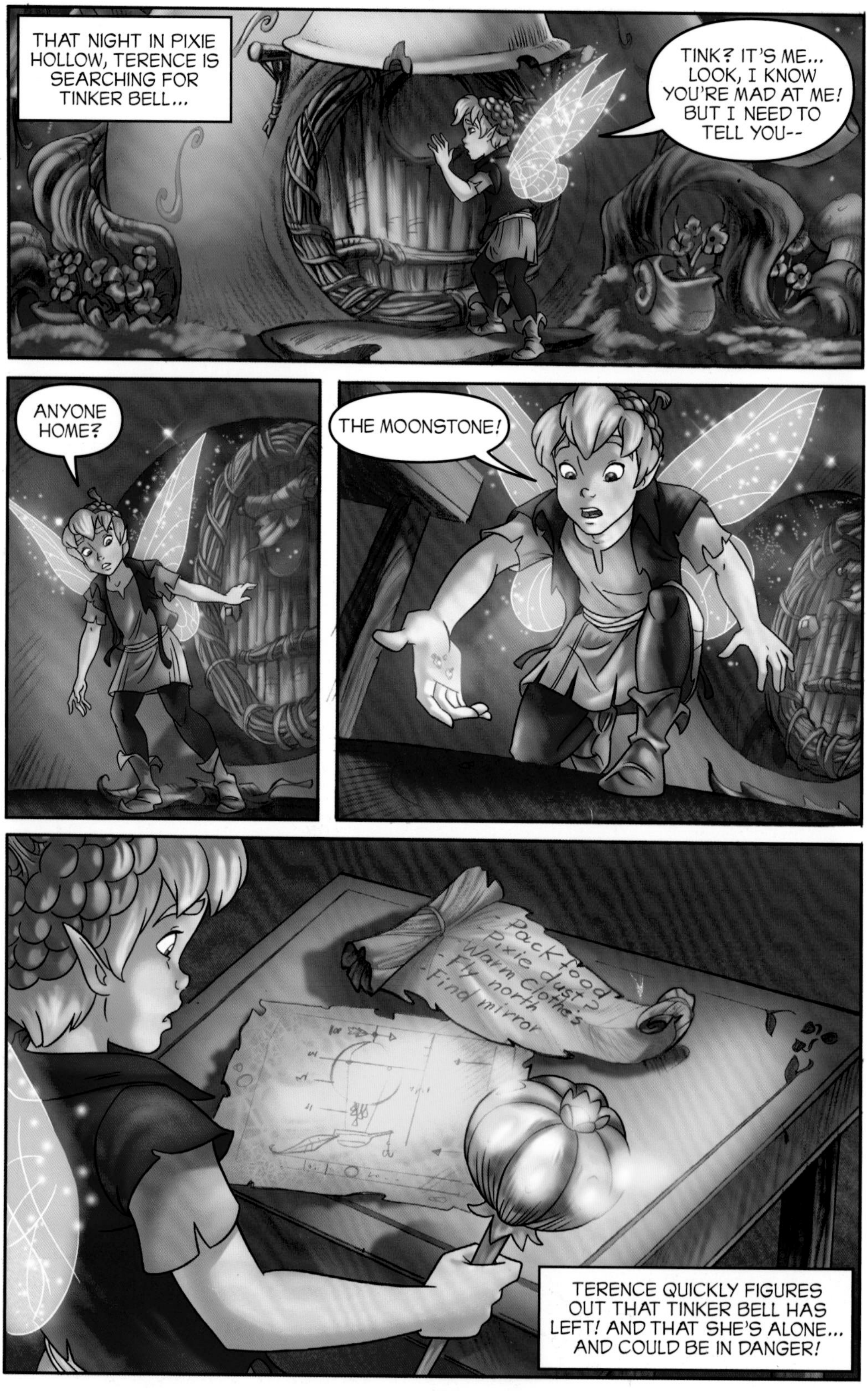
THAT NIGHT IN PIXIE HOLLOW, TERENCE IS SEARCHING FOR TINKER BELL...
TINK? IT'S ME... LOOK, I KNOW YOU'RE MAD AT ME! BUT I NEED TO TELL YOU--
ANYONE HOME?
THE MOONSTONE!
- Pack food
- Pixie dust?
- Warm Clothes
- Fly north
- Find mirror
TERENCE QUICKLY FIGURES OUT THAT TINKER BELL HAS LEFT! AND THAT SHE'S ALONE... AND COULD BE IN DANGER!

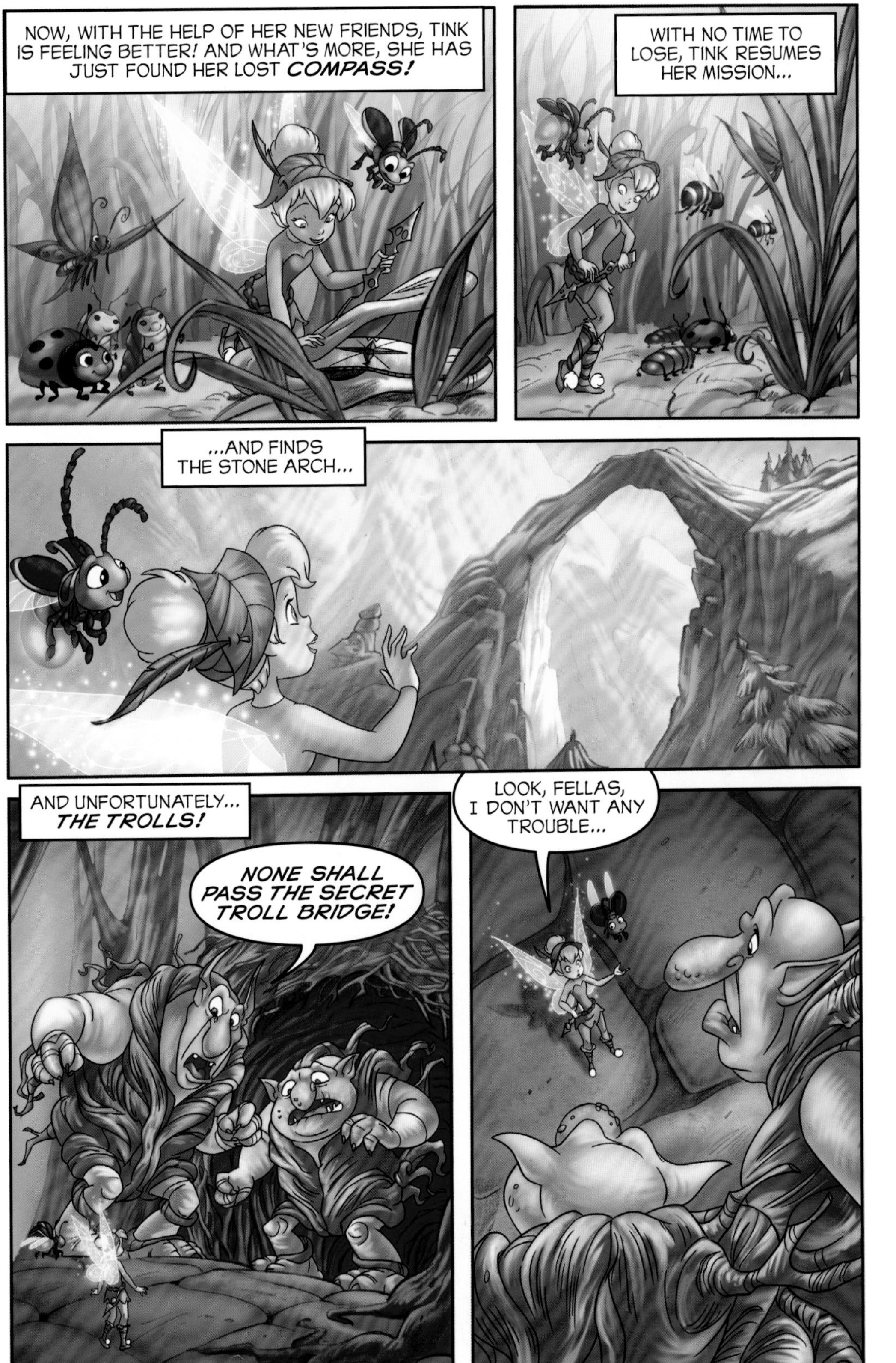
NOW, WITH THE HELP OF HER NEW FRIENDS, TINK IS FEELING BETTER! AND WHAT'S MORE, SHE HAS JUST FOUND HER LOST COMPASS!
WITH NO TIME TO LOSE, TINK RESUMES HER MISSION...
...AND FINDS THE STONE ARCH...
AND UNFORTUNATELY... THE TROLLS!
NONE SHALL PASS THE SECRET TROLL BRIDGE!
LOOK, FELLAS, I DON'T WANT ANY TROUBLE...

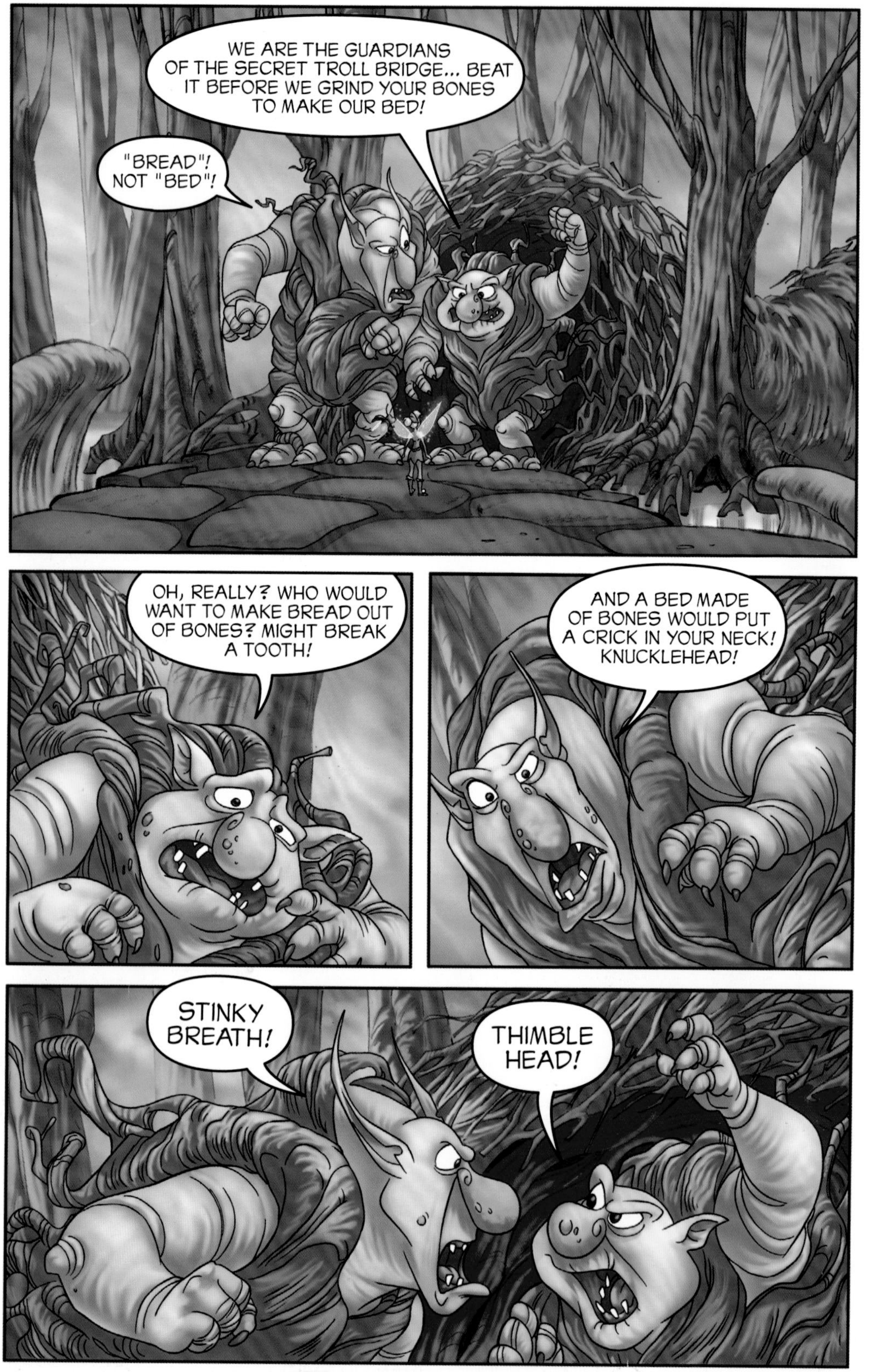
WE ARE THE GUARDIANS OF THE SECRET TROLL BRIDGE... BEAT IT BEFORE WE GRIND YOUR BONES TO MAKE OUR BED!
"BREAD"! NOT "BED"!
OH, REALLY? WHO WOULD WANT TO MAKE BREAD OUT OF BONES? MIGHT BREAK A TOOTH!
AND A BED MADE OF BONES WOULD PUT A CRICK IN YOUR NECK! KNUCKLEHEAD!
STINKY BREATH!
THIMBLE HEAD!

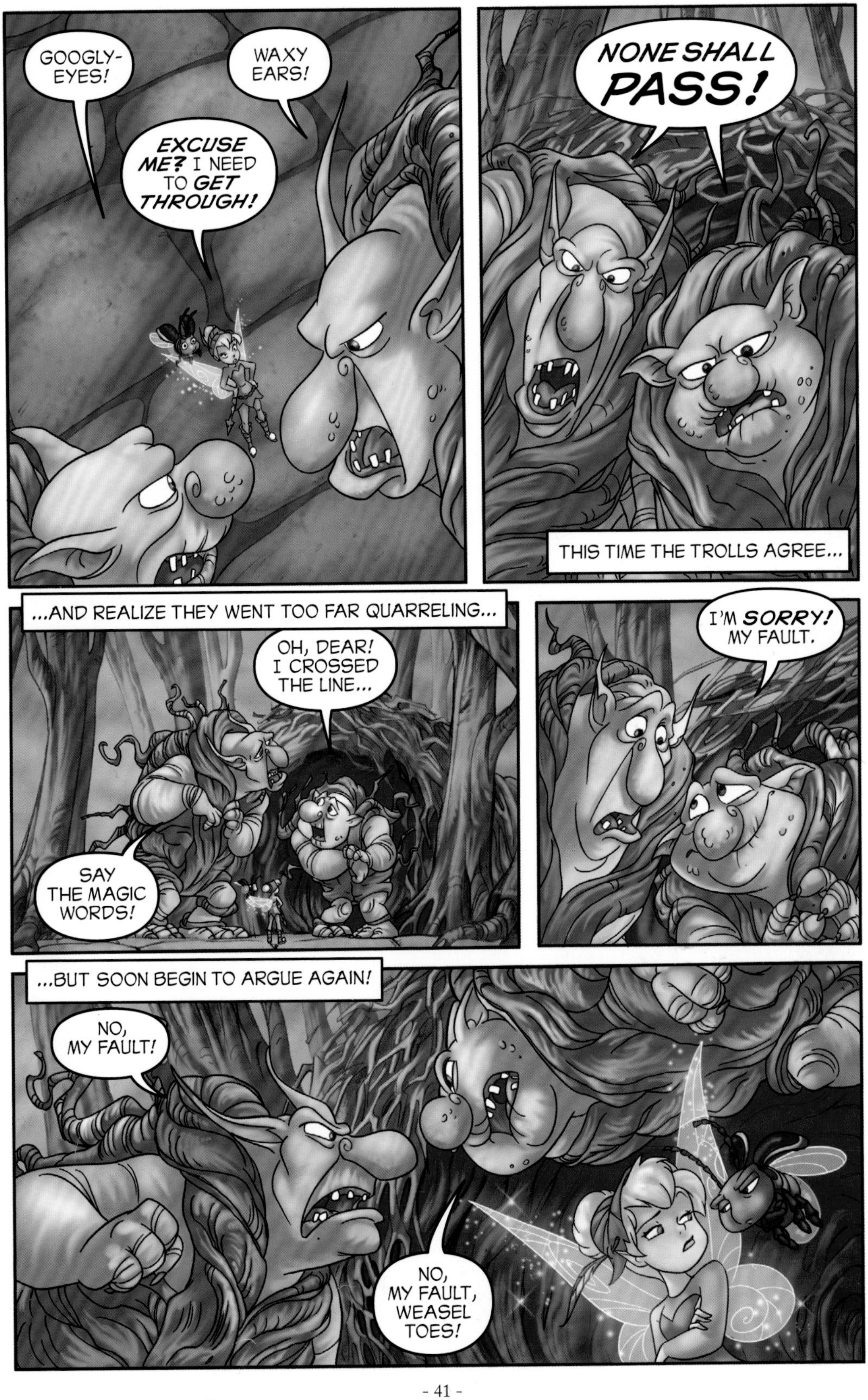
GOOGLY-EYES!
WAXY EARS!
EXCUSE ME? I NEED TO GET THROUGH!
NONE SHALL PASS!
THIS TIME THE TROLLS AGREE...
...AND REALIZE THEY WENT TOO FAR QUARRELING...
OH, DEAR! I CROSSED THE LINE...
SAY THE MAGIC WORDS!
I'M SORRY! MY FAULT.
...BUT SOON BEGIN TO ARGUE AGAIN!
NO, MY FAULT!
NO, MY FAULT, WEASEL TOES!

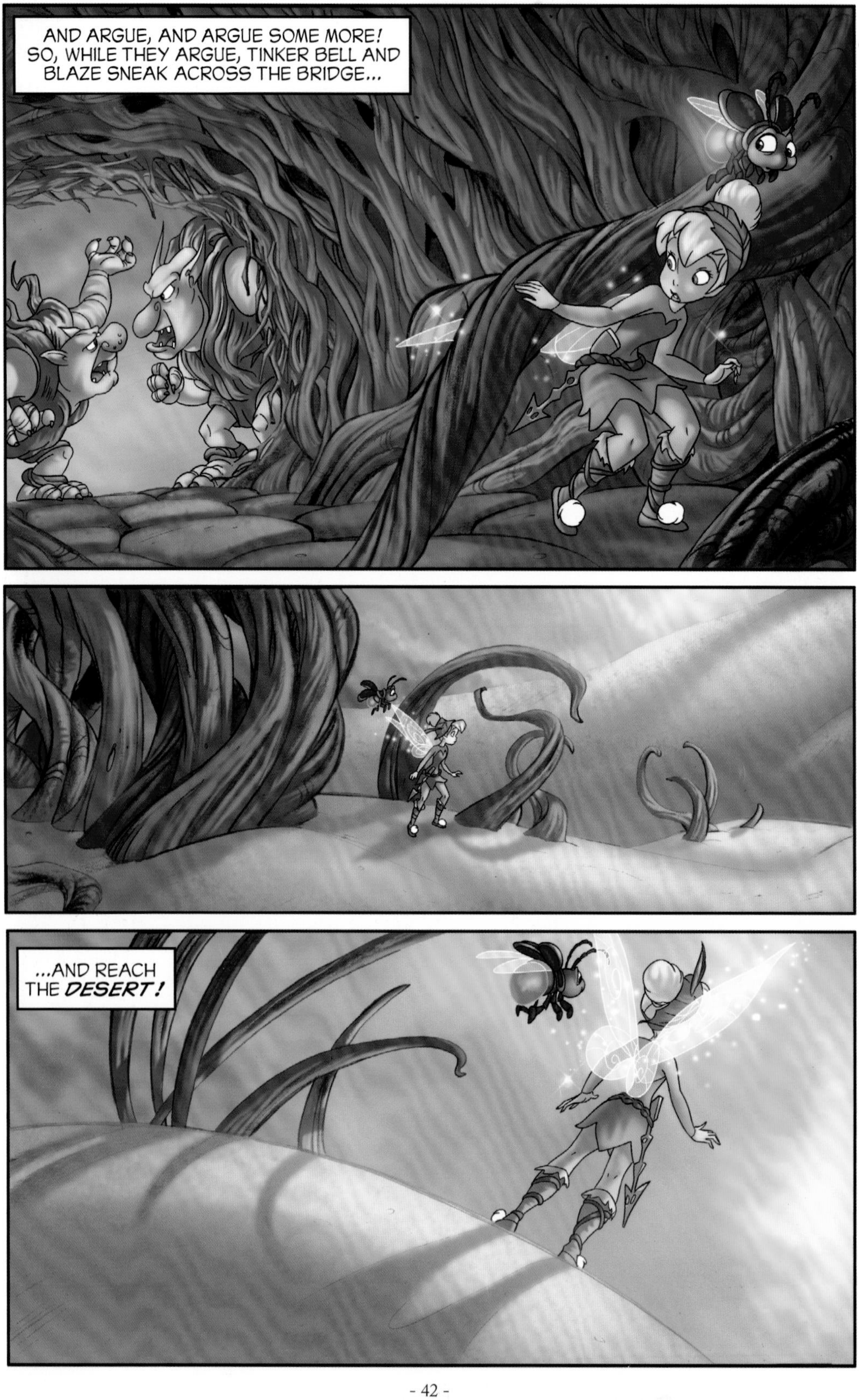
AND ARGUE, AND ARGUE SOME MORE! SO, WHILE THEY ARGUE, TINKER BELL AND BLAZE SNEAK ACROSS THE BRIDGE...
...AND REACH THE DESERT!

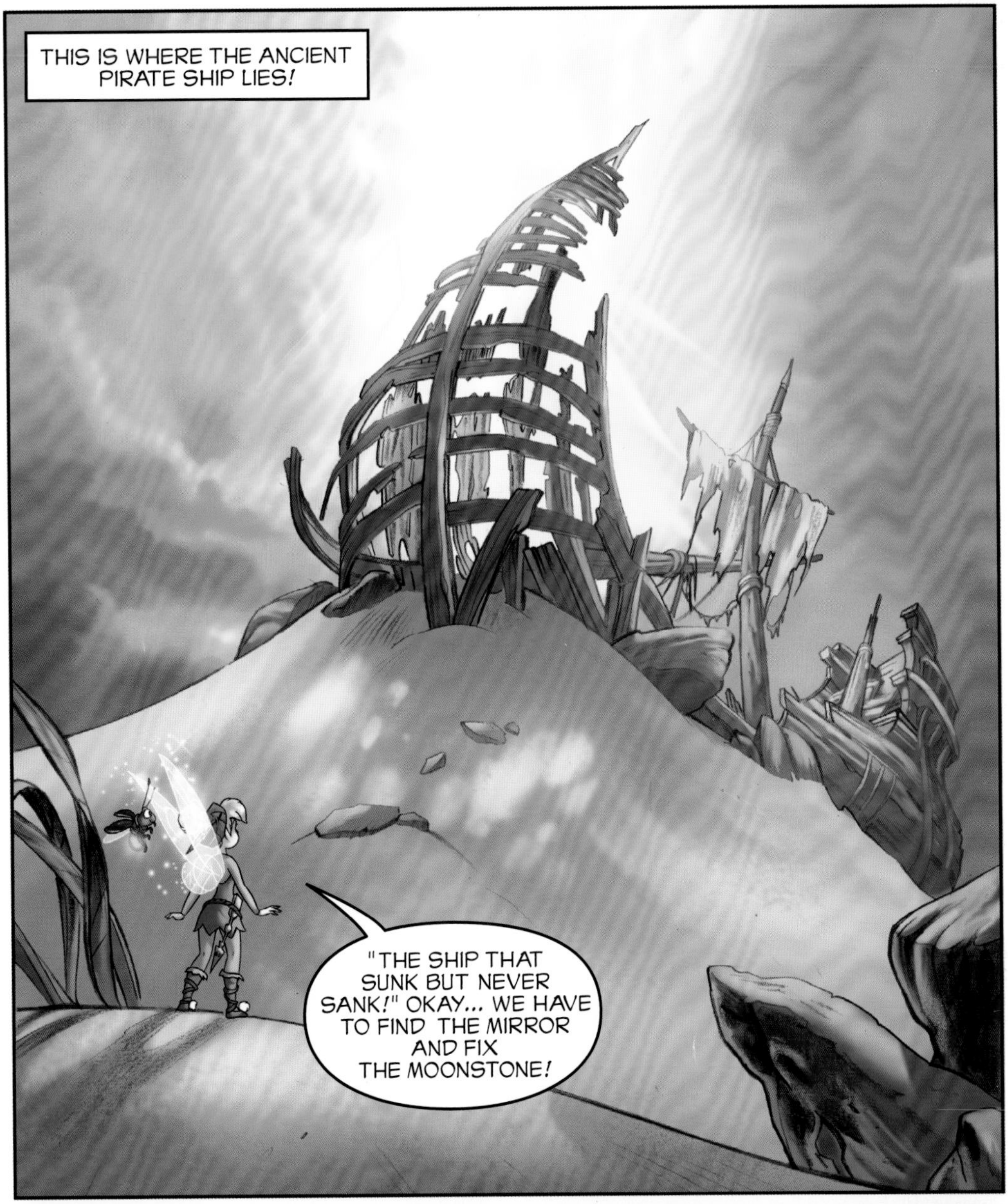
THIS IS WHERE THE ANCIENT PIRATE SHIP LIES!
"THE SHIP THAT SUNK BUT NEVER SANK!" OKAY... WE HAVE TO FIND THE MIRROR AND FIX THE MOONSTONE!

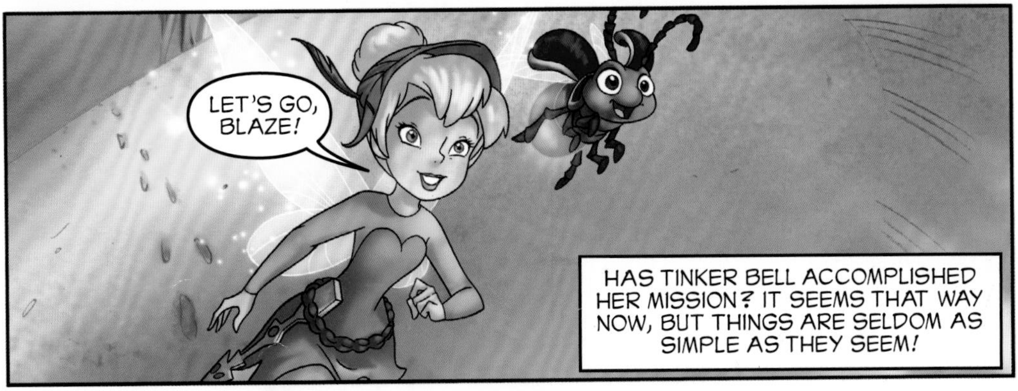
LET'S GO, BLAZE!
HAS TINKER BELL ACCOMPLISHED HER MISSION? IT SEEMS THAT WAY NOW, BUT THINGS ARE SELDOM AS SIMPLE AS THEY SEEM!

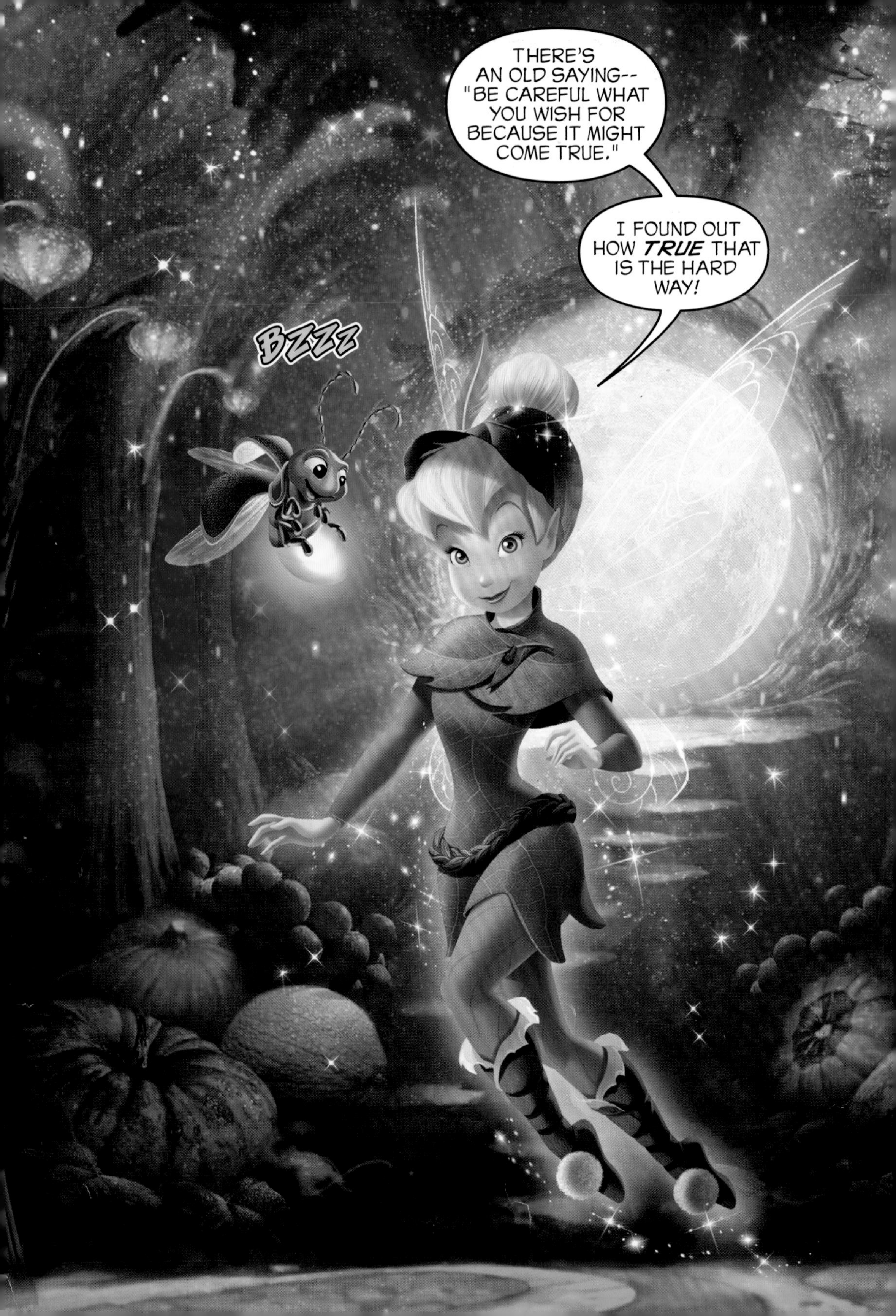
THERE'S AN OLD SAYING-- "BE CAREFUL WHAT YOU WISH FOR BECAUSE IT MIGHT COME TRUE."
I FOUND OUT HOW *TRUE* THAT IS THE HARD WAY!
BZZz

THE GLOW OF FRIENDSHIP

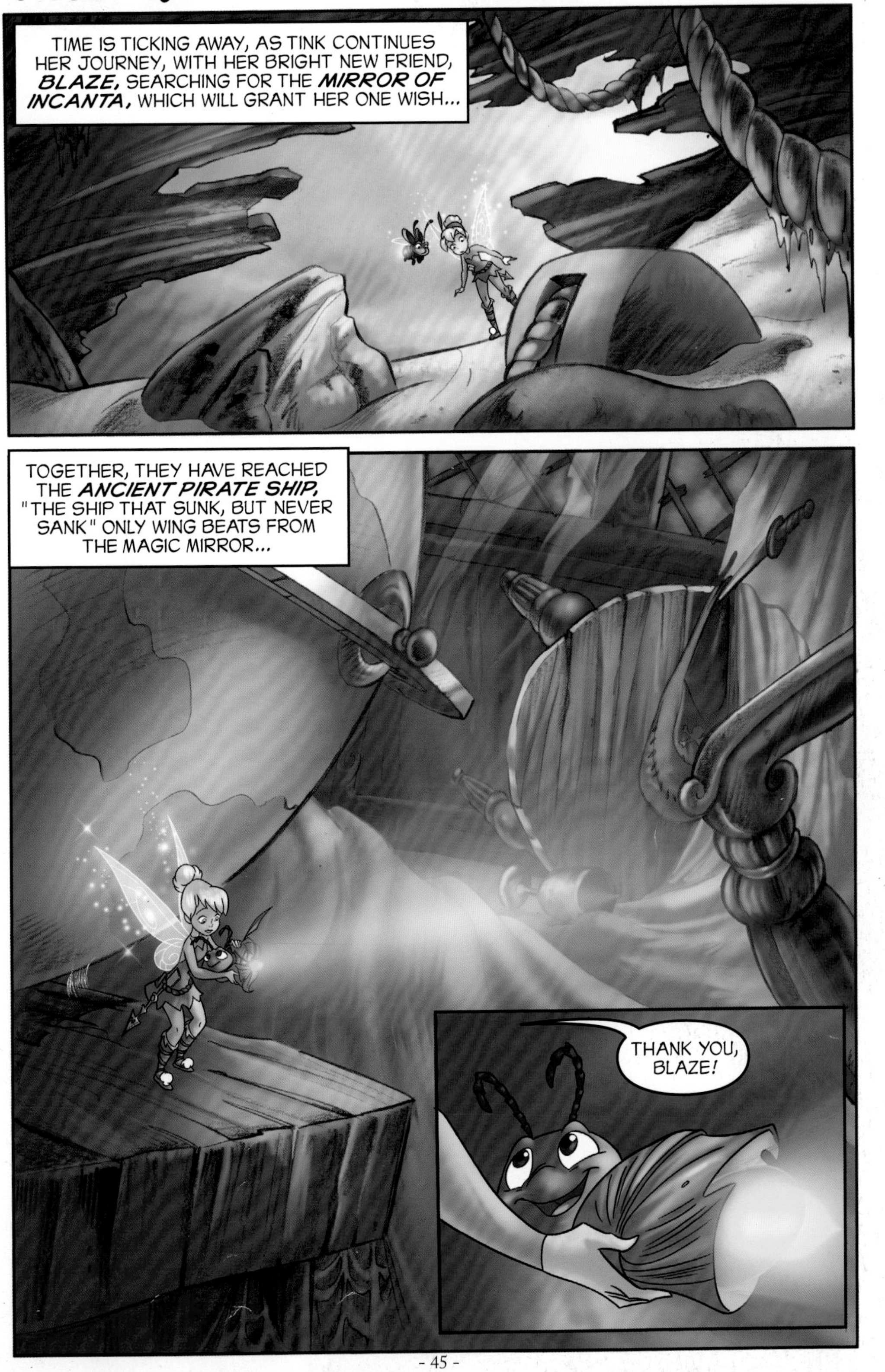

TIME IS TICKING AWAY, AS TINK CONTINUES HER JOURNEY, WITH HER BRIGHT NEW FRIEND, BLAZE, SEARCHING FOR THE MIRROR OF INCANTA, WHICH WILL GRANT HER ONE WISH...
TOGETHER, THEY HAVE REACHED THE ANCIENT PIRATE SHIP, "THE SHIP THAT SUNK, BUT NEVER SANK" ONLY WING BEATS FROM THE MAGIC MIRROR...
THANK YOU, BLAZE!

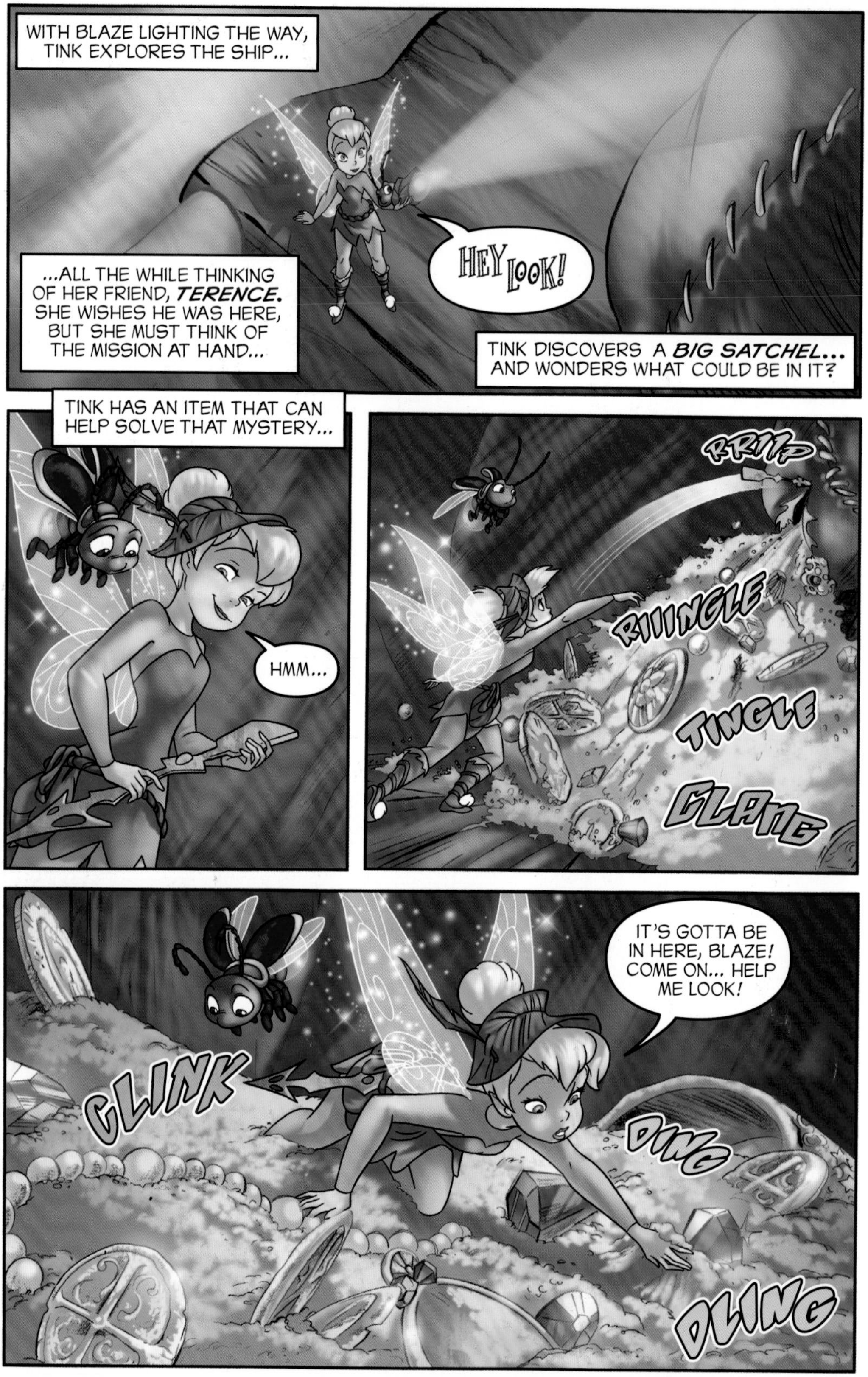
WITH BLAZE LIGHTING THE WAY, TINK EXPLORES THE SHIP...
HEY LOOK!
...ALL THE WHILE THINKING OF HER FRIEND, ***TERENCE.*** SHE WISHES HE WAS HERE, BUT SHE MUST THINK OF THE MISSION AT HAND...
TINK DISCOVERS A ***BIG SATCHEL...*** AND WONDERS WHAT COULD BE IN IT?
TINK HAS AN ITEM THAT CAN HELP SOLVE THAT MYSTERY...
HMM...
RRIIP
RIIINGLE
TINGLE
CLANG
IT'S GOTTA BE IN HERE, BLAZE! COME ON... HELP ME LOOK!
CLINK
DING
DLING

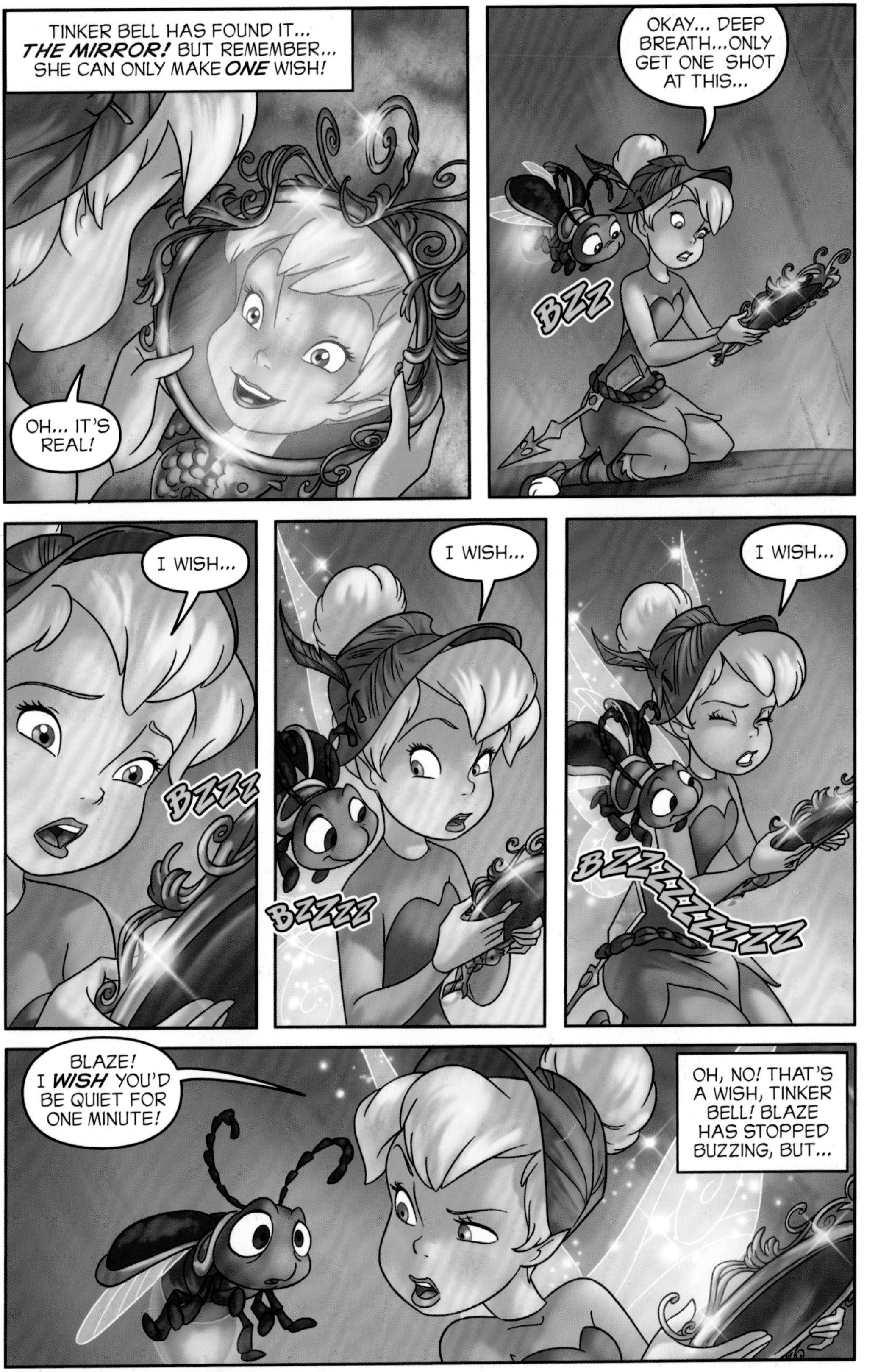

TINKER BELL HAS FOUND IT... THE MIRROR! BUT REMEMBER... SHE CAN ONLY MAKE ONE WISH!
OH... IT'S REAL!
OKAY... DEEP BREATH...ONLY GET ONE SHOT AT THIS...
BZZ
I WISH...
BZZZ
I WISH...
BZZZZ
I WISH...
BZZZZZZZZZZZZ
BLAZE! I WISH YOU'D BE QUIET FOR ONE MINUTE!
OH, NO! THAT'S A WISH, TINKER BELL! BLAZE HAS STOPPED BUZZING, BUT...

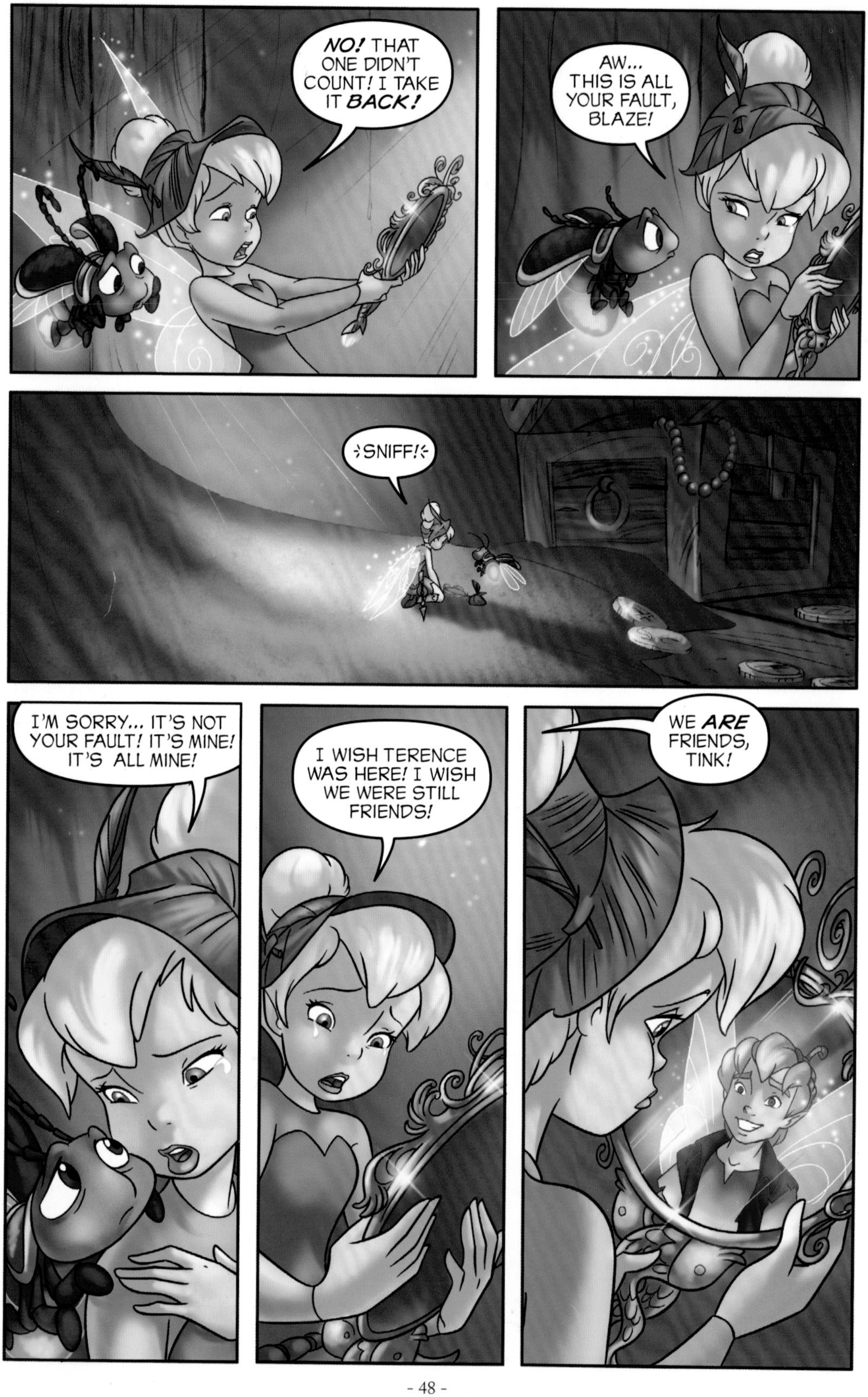
NO! THAT ONE DIDN'T COUNT! I TAKE IT BACK!
AW... THIS IS ALL YOUR FAULT, BLAZE!
SNIFF!
I'M SORRY... IT'S NOT YOUR FAULT! IT'S MINE! IT'S ALL MINE!
I WISH TERENCE WAS HERE! I WISH WE WERE STILL FRIENDS!
WE ARE FRIENDS, TINK!

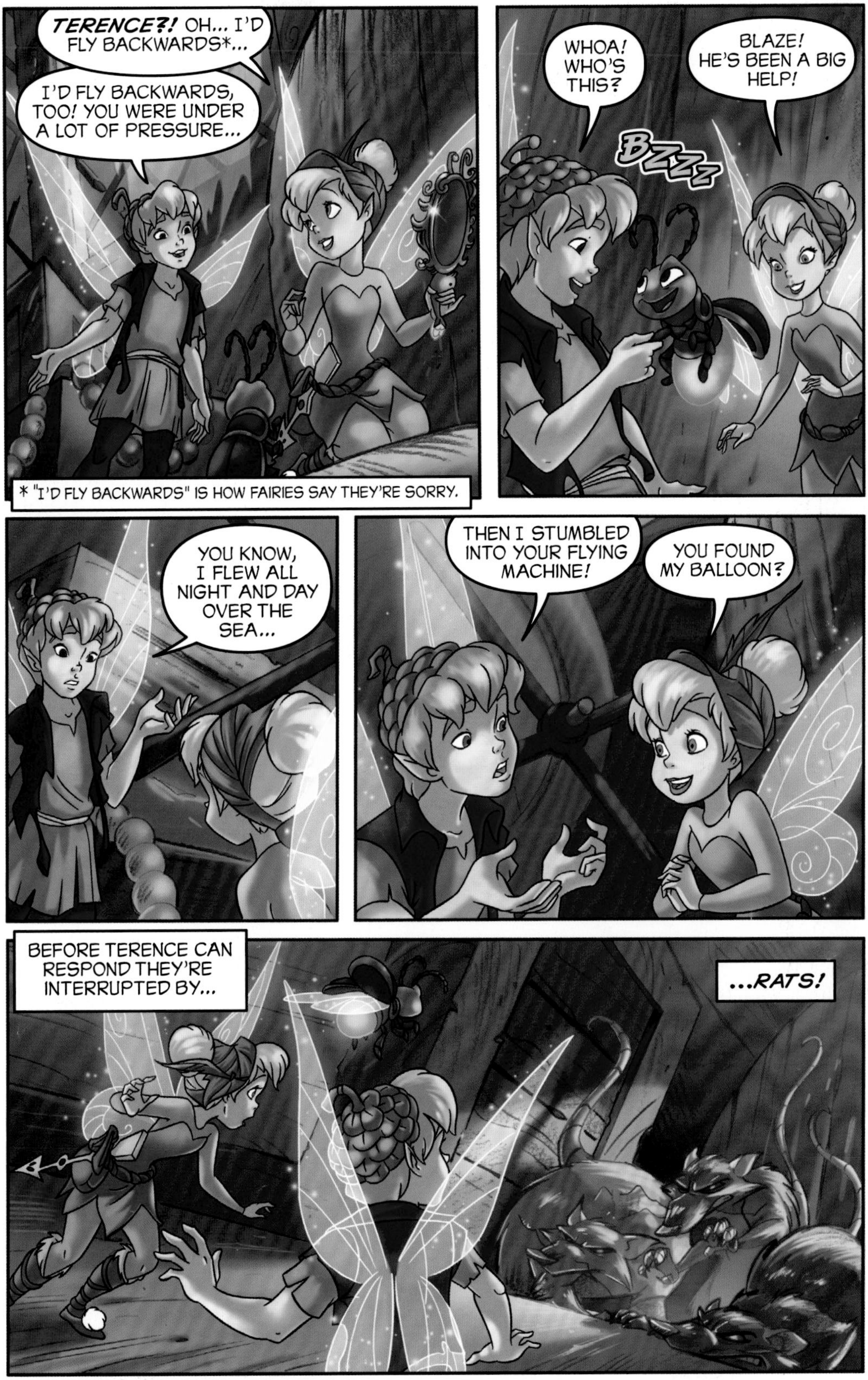
TERENCE?! OH... I'D FLY BACKWARDS*...
I'D FLY BACKWARDS, TOO! YOU WERE UNDER A LOT OF PRESSURE...
* "I'D FLY BACKWARDS" IS HOW FAIRIES SAY THEY'RE SORRY.
WHOA! WHO'S THIS?
BLAZE! HE'S BEEN A BIG HELP!
BZZZ
YOU KNOW, I FLEW ALL NIGHT AND DAY OVER THE SEA...
THEN I STUMBLED INTO YOUR FLYING MACHINE!
YOU FOUND MY BALLOON?
BEFORE TERENCE CAN RESPOND THEY'RE INTERRUPTED BY...
...RATS!

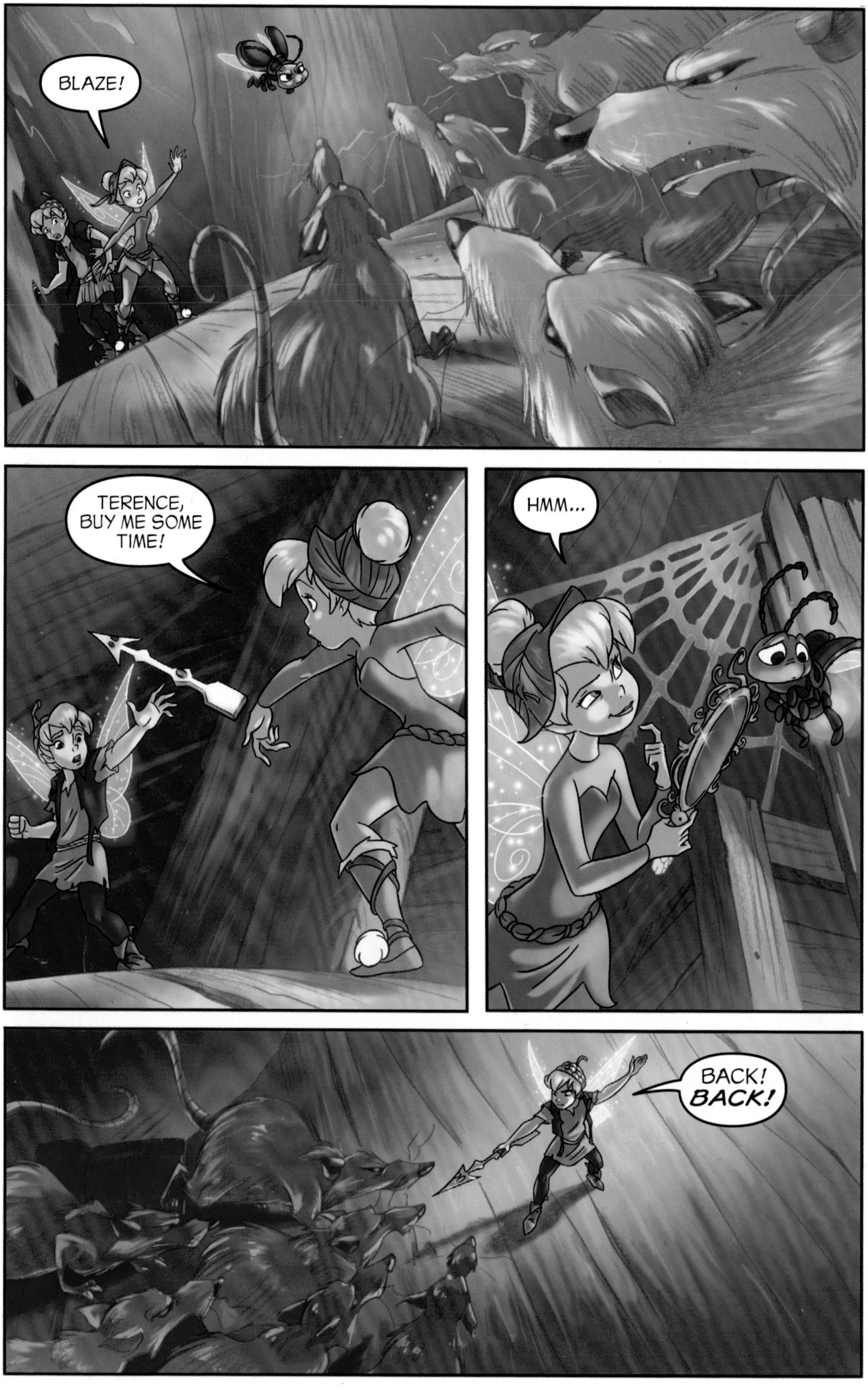
BLAZE!
TERENCE, BUY ME SOME TIME!
HMM...
BACK! BACK!

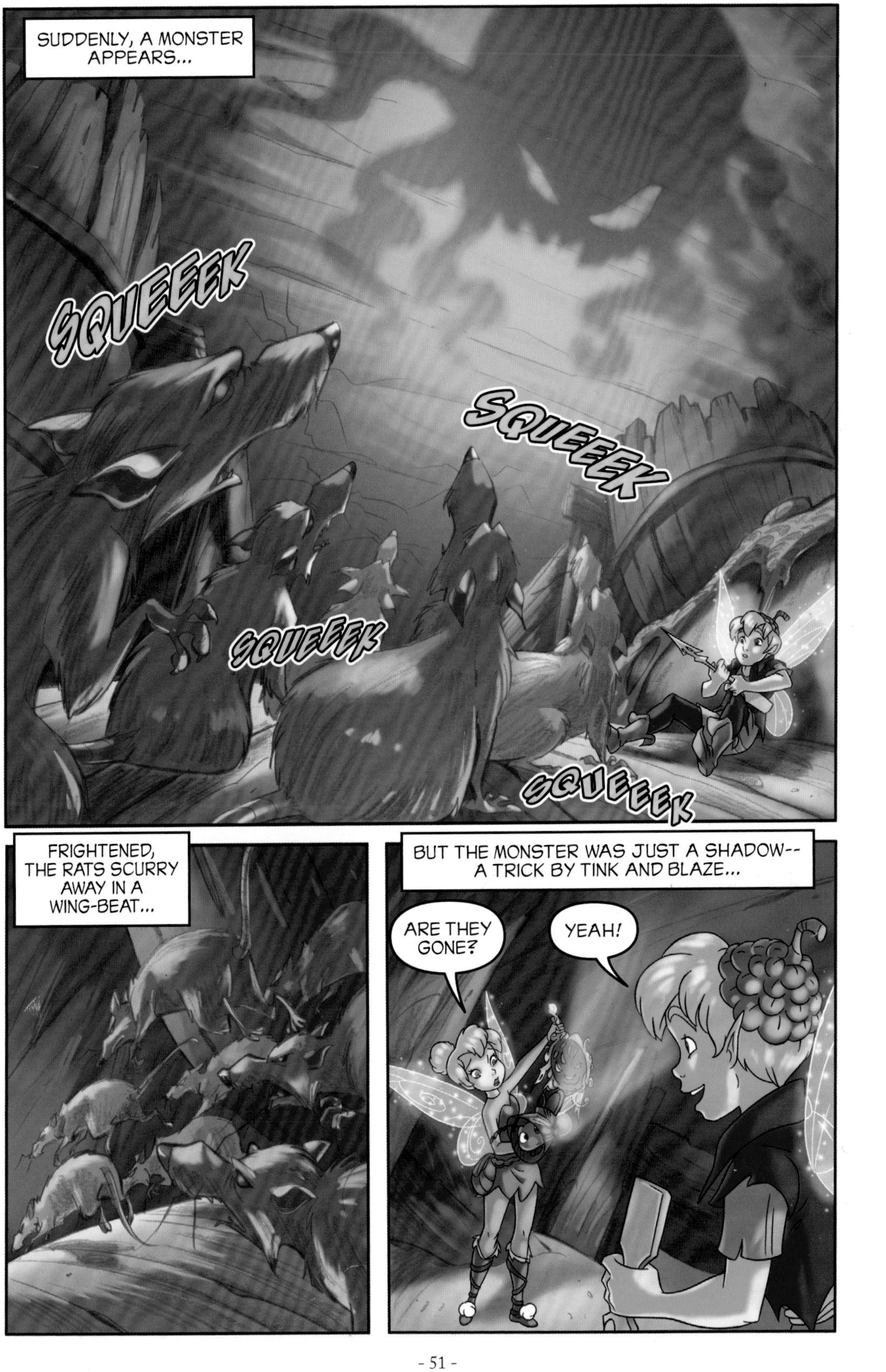
SUDDENLY, A MONSTER APPEARS...
SQUEEEK
SQUEEEEK
SQUEEEK
SQUEEEK
FRIGHTENED, THE RATS SCURRY AWAY IN A WING-BEAT...
BUT THE MONSTER WAS JUST A SHADOW-- A TRICK BY TINK AND BLAZE...
ARE THEY GONE?
YEAH!

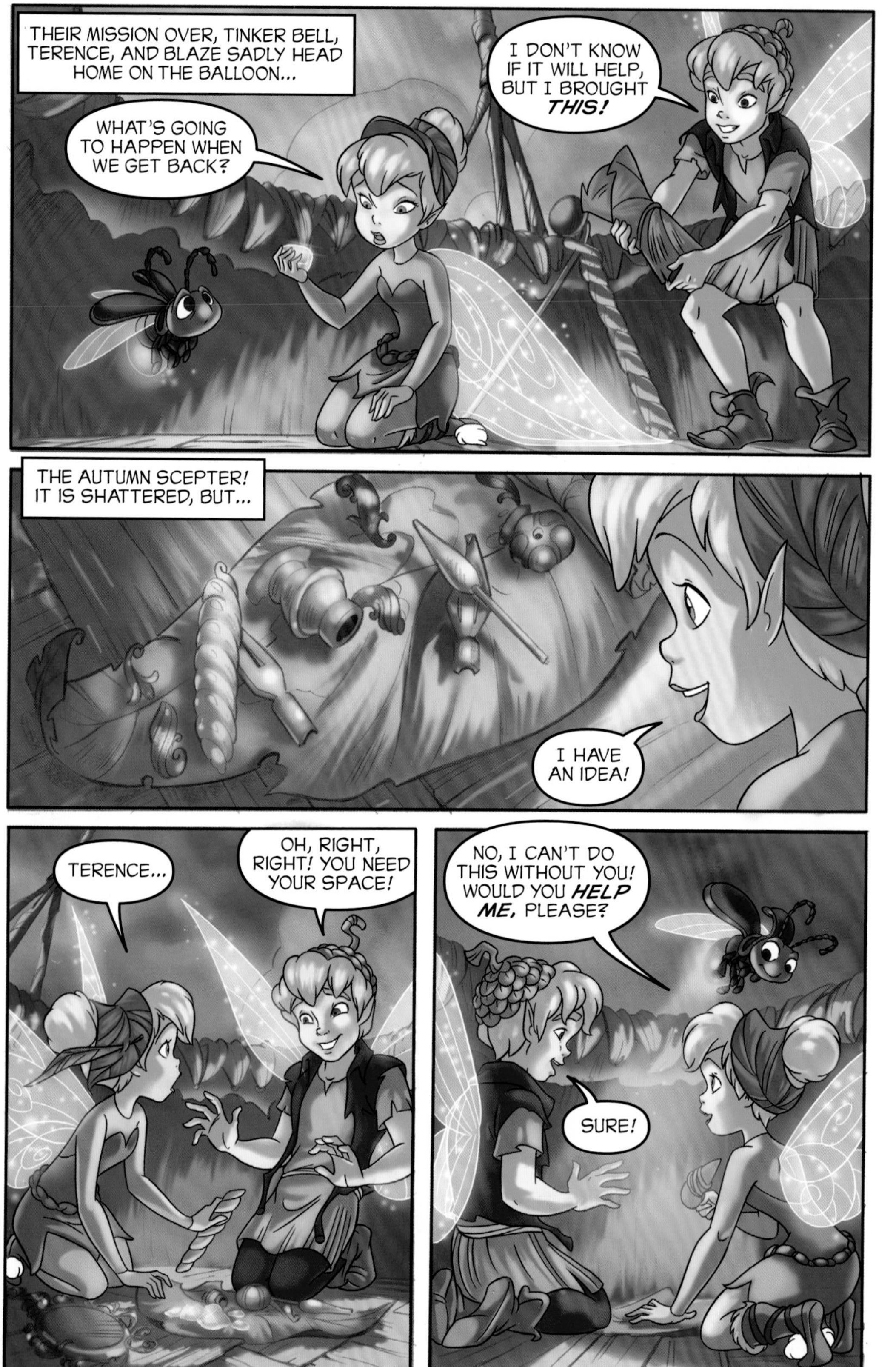
THEIR MISSION OVER, TINKER BELL, TERENCE, AND BLAZE SADLY HEAD HOME ON THE BALLOON...
WHAT'S GOING TO HAPPEN WHEN WE GET BACK?
I DON'T KNOW IF IT WILL HELP, BUT I BROUGHT *THIS!*
THE AUTUMN SCEPTER! IT IS SHATTERED, BUT...
I HAVE AN IDEA!
TERENCE...
OH, RIGHT, RIGHT! YOU NEED YOUR SPACE!
NO, I CAN'T DO THIS WITHOUT YOU! WOULD YOU *HELP ME,* PLEASE?
SURE!

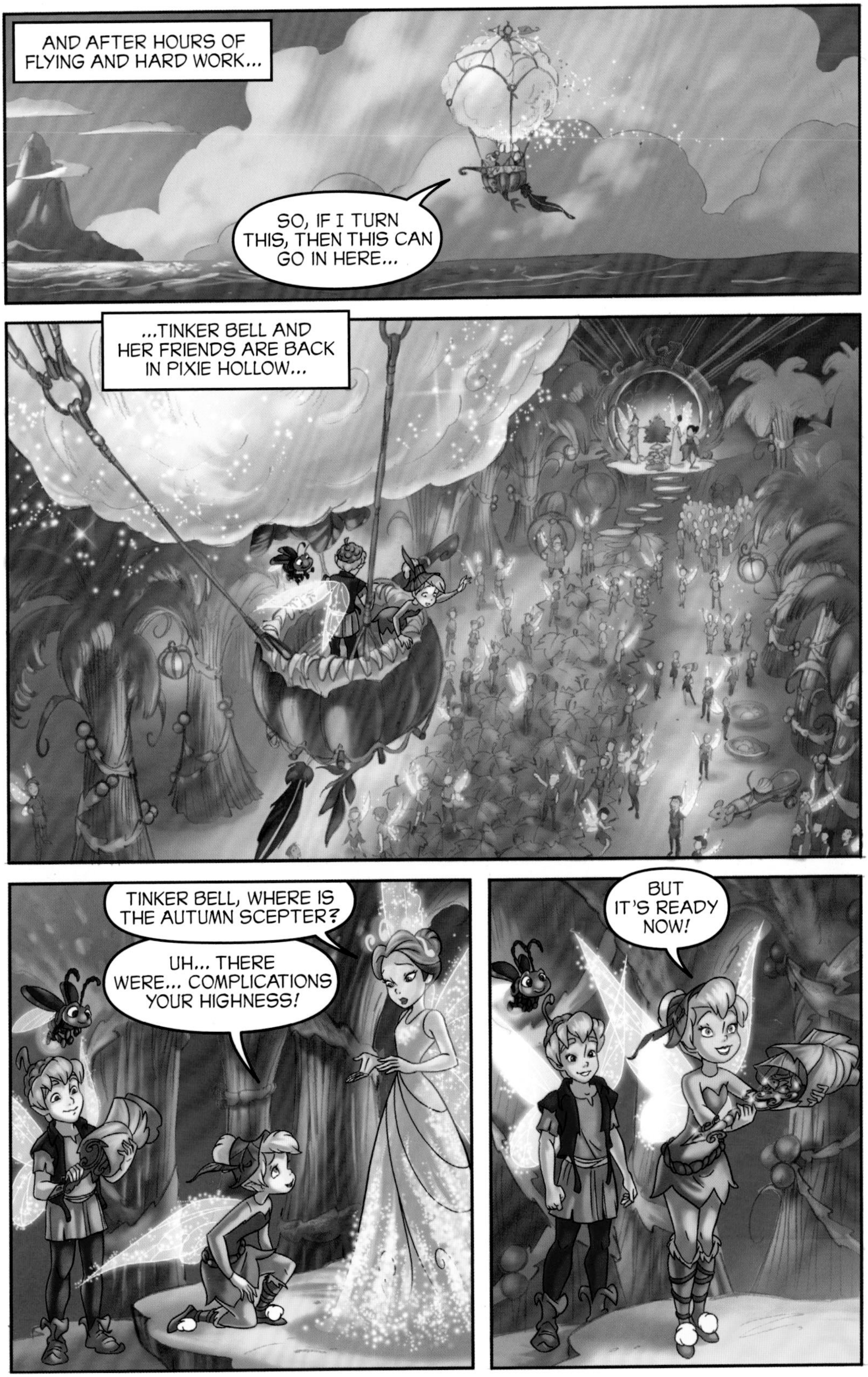
AND AFTER HOURS OF FLYING AND HARD WORK...
SO, IF I TURN THIS, THEN THIS CAN GO IN HERE...
...TINKER BELL AND HER FRIENDS ARE BACK IN PIXIE HOLLOW...
TINKER BELL, WHERE IS THE AUTUMN SCEPTER?
UH... THERE WERE... COMPLICATIONS YOUR HIGHNESS!
BUT IT'S READY NOW!

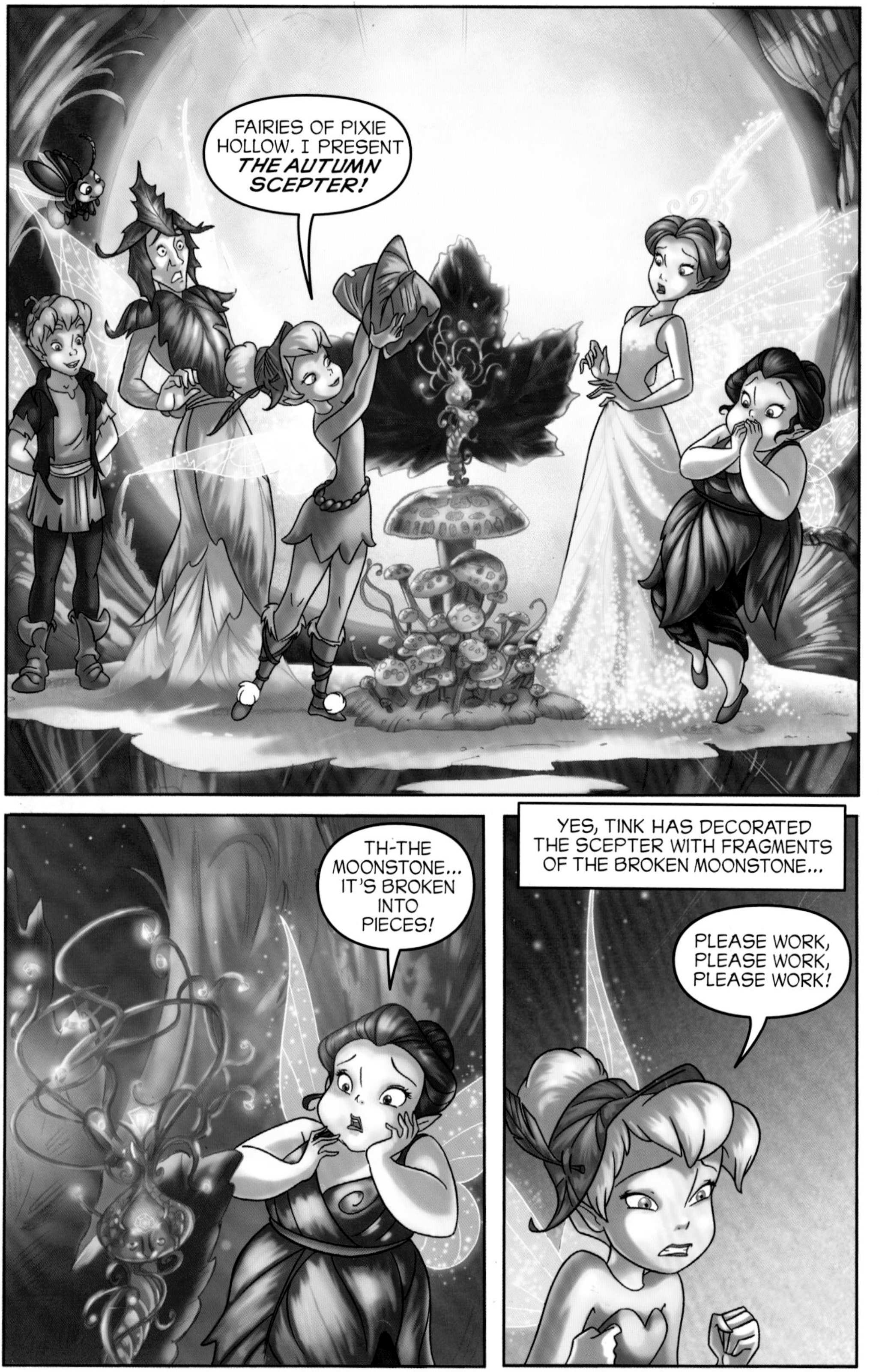
FAIRIES OF PIXIE HOLLOW. I PRESENT *THE AUTUMN SCEPTER!*
TH-THE MOONSTONE... IT'S BROKEN INTO PIECES!
YES, TINK HAS DECORATED THE SCEPTER WITH FRAGMENTS OF THE BROKEN MOONSTONE...
PLEASE WORK, PLEASE WORK, PLEASE WORK!

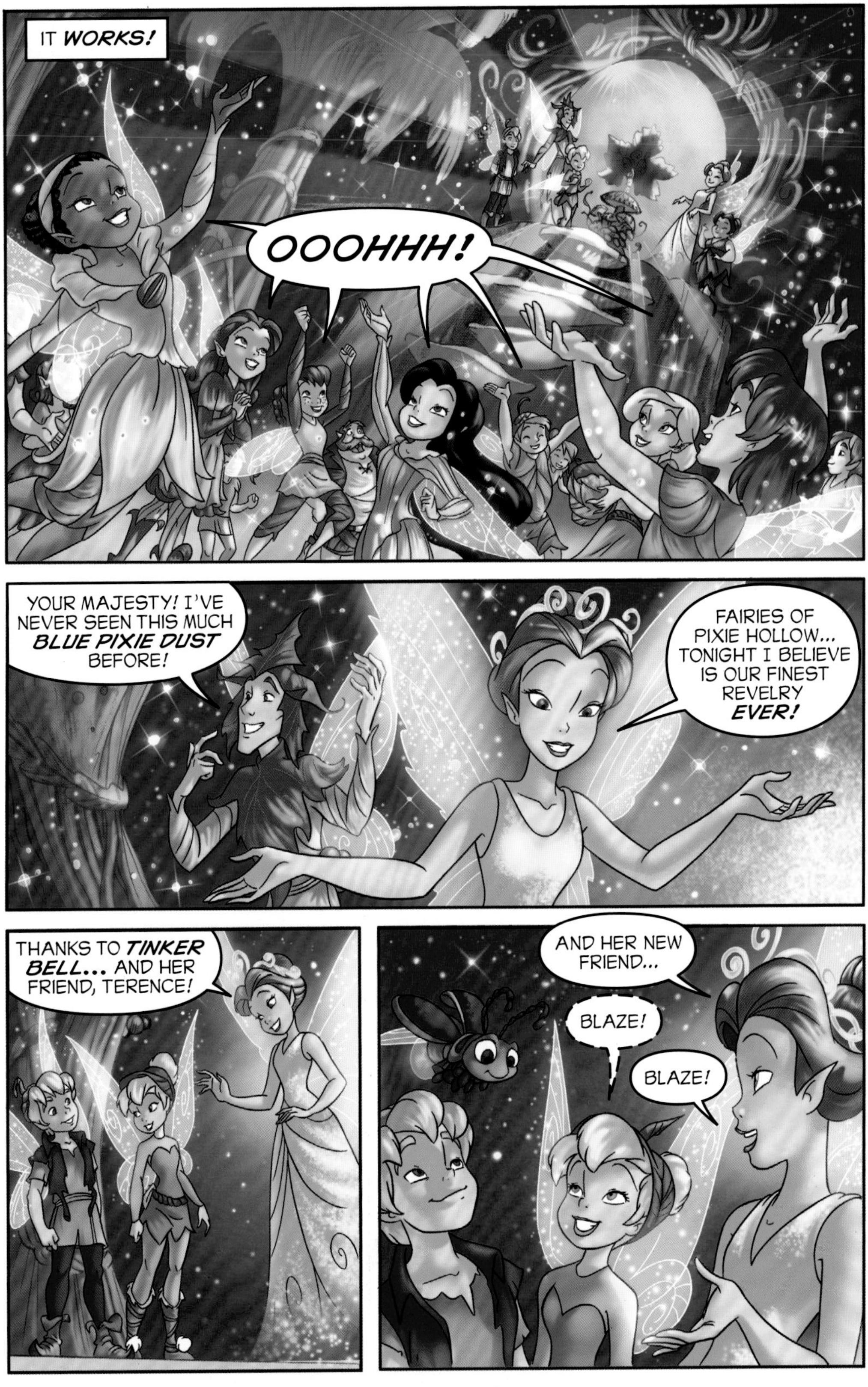
IT WORKS!
OOOHHH!
YOUR MAJESTY! I'VE NEVER SEEN THIS MUCH BLUE PIXIE DUST BEFORE!
FAIRIES OF PIXIE HOLLOW... TONIGHT I BELIEVE IS OUR FINEST REVELRY EVER!
THANKS TO TINKER BELL... AND HER FRIEND, TERENCE!
AND HER NEW FRIEND...
BLAZE!
BLAZE!

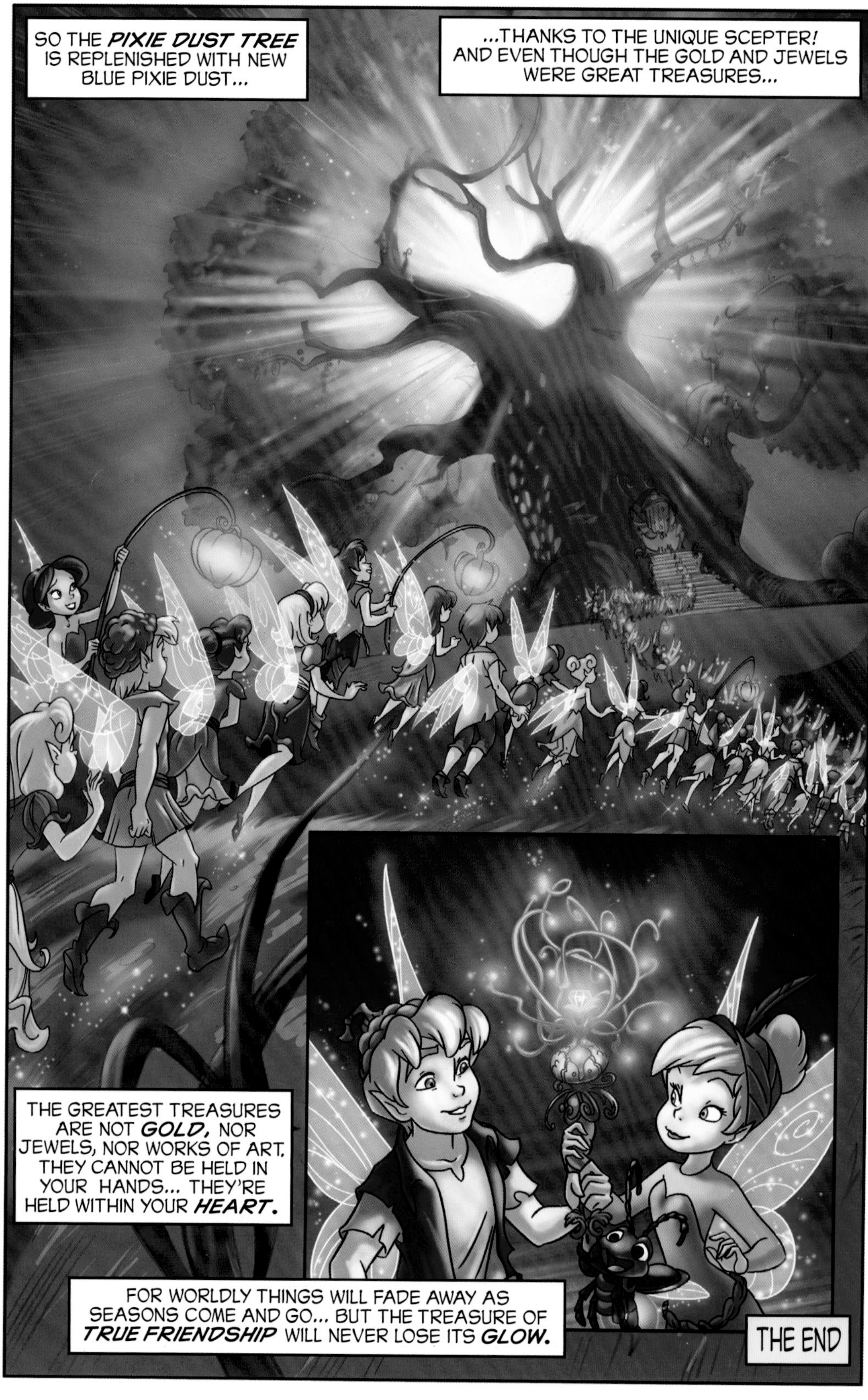
SO THE *PIXIE DUST TREE* IS REPLENISHED WITH NEW BLUE PIXIE DUST...
...THANKS TO THE UNIQUE SCEPTER! AND EVEN THOUGH THE GOLD AND JEWELS WERE GREAT TREASURES...
THE GREATEST TREASURES ARE NOT **GOLD,** NOR JEWELS, NOR WORKS OF ART. THEY CANNOT BE HELD IN YOUR HANDS... THEY'RE HELD WITHIN YOUR **HEART.**
FOR WORLDLY THINGS WILL FADE AWAY AS SEASONS COME AND GO... BUT THE TREASURE OF **TRUE FRIENDSHIP** WILL NEVER LOSE ITS **GLOW.**
THE END

WATCH OUT FOR PAPERCUTZ™

Welcome to the twelfth treasure-filled DISNEY FAIRIES graphic novel from Papercutz, those kids who refuse to ever grow up, dedicated to publishing great graphic novels for all ages! I'm Jim Salicrup, the Editor-in-Chief and professional Pixie Dust distributor.

Recently, I attended the birthday party for Cortney Faye Powell, who contributes revised dialogue and captions to DISNEY FAIRIES, and thought I'd share this pic of the lovely coconut birthday cake baked by her mom, the multi-talented Paulette Powell.

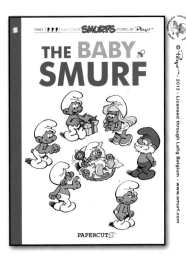

And, yes, it tasted as good as it looks!

In "The Scepter," there's a lot of talk about the Blue Moon! We learn that when the rays of the Blue Moon pass through the moonstone it creates Blue Pixie Dust that restores the Pixie Dust Tree! But it seems that's not all that happens when there's a full moon! According to Papa Smurf, "when the moon's blue, sometimes an extraordinary event can smurf, like for example, the coming of Baby Smurf!" For the full story, look for THE SMURFS #14 "The Baby Smurf," also from Papercutz.

In "The Glow of Friendship," Tinker Bell gets the opportunity to make a wish. Too bad she didn't wish for the Genie from Aladdin-- then she would've had a lot of wishes! In THE GARFIELD SHOW #1 "Unfair Weather," Garfield's friend Odie finds a genie in a bottle on the beach. Garfield thinks he has it all figured out, when he thinks, "I know exactly what my first wish would be. I would wish for a million more wishes. And just before I use all of them up, I'd wish for another million and then another, and then another..." Me? I just wish you'll come back and enjoy DISNEY FAIRIES #13 "Tinker Bell and the Pixie Hollow Games." Check out the special preview in a couple of pages. What do you wish for? Whatever it is, remember to keep believing in "faith, trust, and Pixie Dust"! It can't hurt!

Thanks,

Jim

THREE FULL-COLOR SMURFS STORIES BY Peyo
THE BABY SMURF
PAPERCUTZ

5 STORIES BASED UPON ORIGINAL CHARACTERS BY JIM DAVIS
The GARFIELD Show
UNFAIR WEATHER
PAPERCUTZ

STAY IN TOUCH!

EMAIL: salicrup@papercutz.com
WEB: www.papercutz.com
TWITTER: @papercutzgn
FACEBOOK: PAPERCUTZGRAPHICNOVELS
REGULAR MAIL: Papercutz, 160 Broadway, Suite 700, East Wing, New York, NY 10038

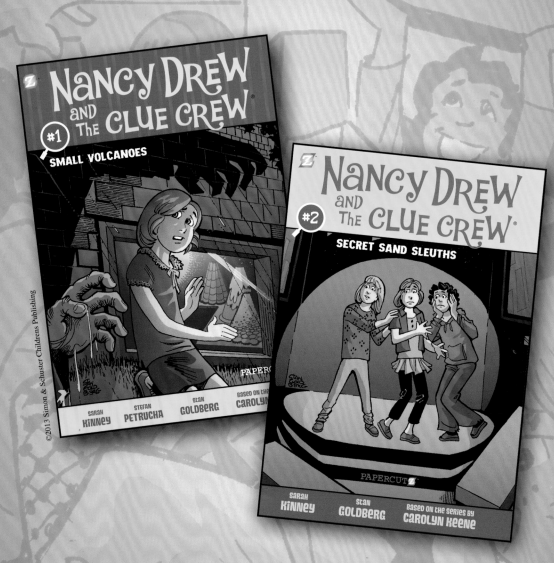

Special Preview of DISNEY FAIRIES #13 "Tinker Bell and the Pixie Hollow Games"...

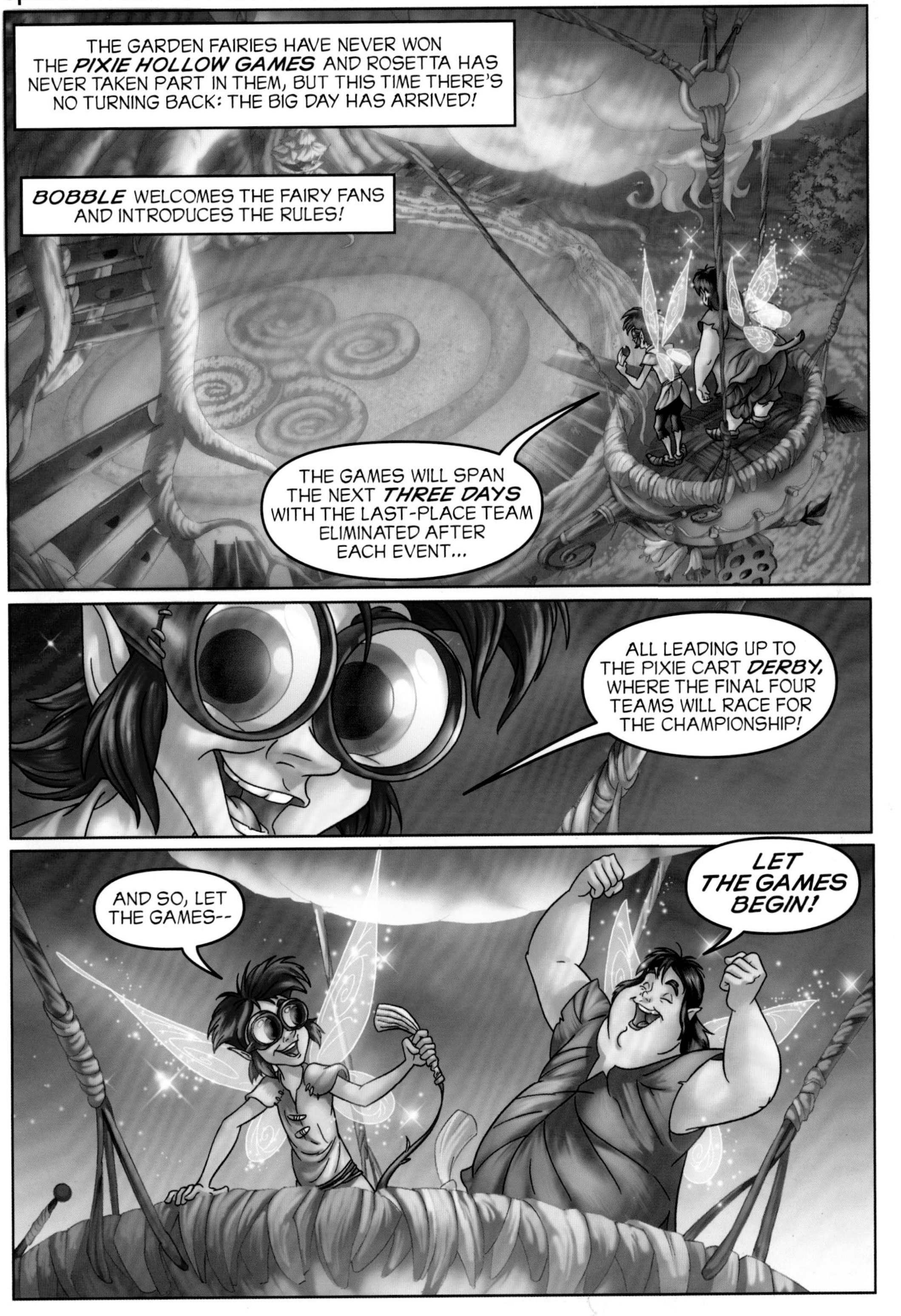
THE GARDEN FAIRIES HAVE NEVER WON THE PIXIE HOLLOW GAMES AND ROSETTA HAS NEVER TAKEN PART IN THEM, BUT THIS TIME THERE'S NO TURNING BACK: THE BIG DAY HAS ARRIVED!
BOBBLE WELCOMES THE FAIRY FANS AND INTRODUCES THE RULES!
THE GAMES WILL SPAN THE NEXT THREE DAYS WITH THE LAST-PLACE TEAM ELIMINATED AFTER EACH EVENT...
ALL LEADING UP TO THE PIXIE CART DERBY, WHERE THE FINAL FOUR TEAMS WILL RACE FOR THE CHAMPIONSHIP!
AND SO, LET THE GAMES--
LET THE GAMES BEGIN!

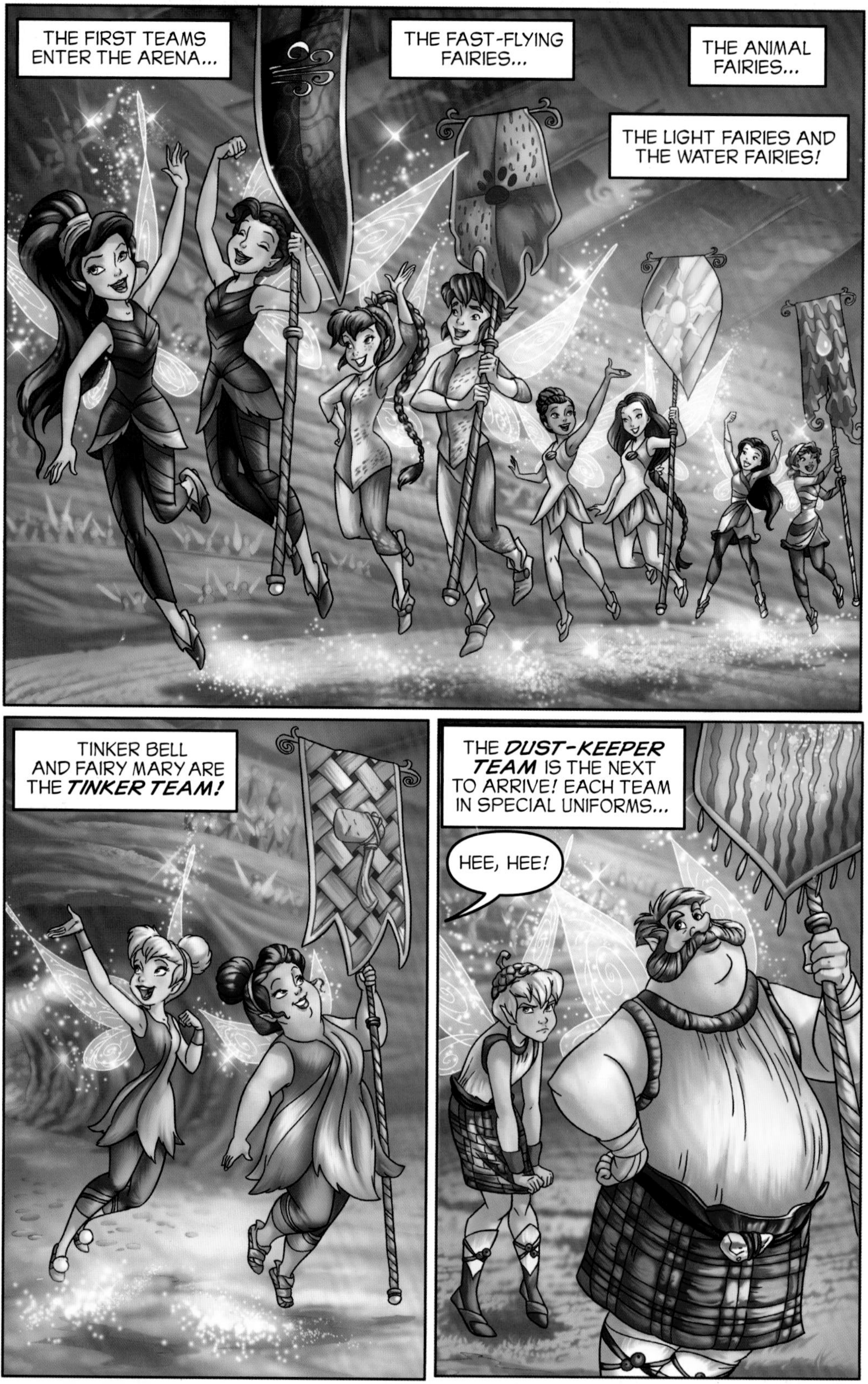
THE FIRST TEAMS ENTER THE ARENA...
THE FAST-FLYING FAIRIES...
THE ANIMAL FAIRIES...
THE LIGHT FAIRIES AND THE WATER FAIRIES!
TINKER BELL AND FAIRY MARY ARE THE TINKER TEAM!
THE DUST-KEEPER TEAM IS THE NEXT TO ARRIVE! EACH TEAM IN SPECIAL UNIFORMS...
HEE, HEE!

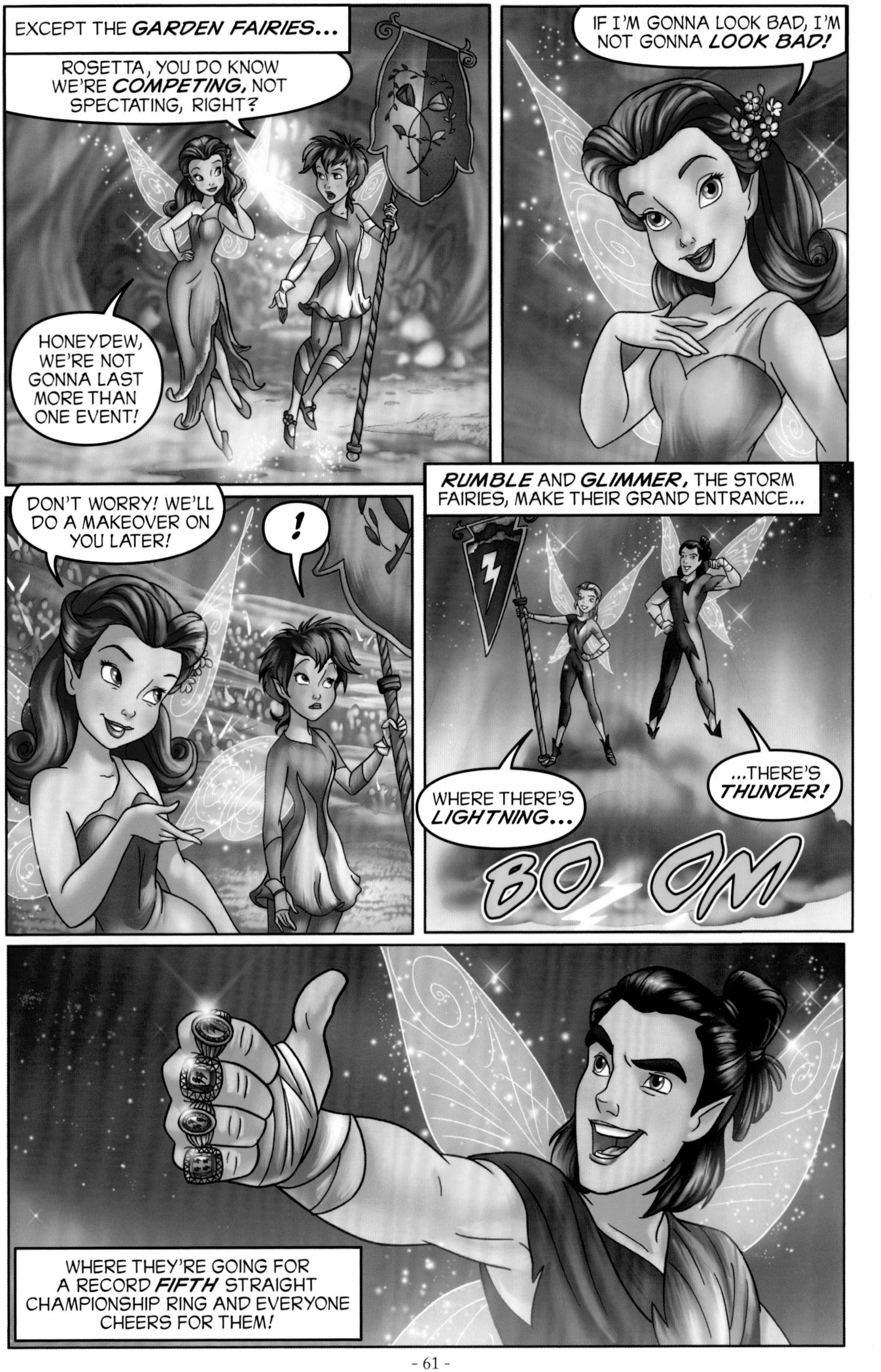

EXCEPT THE GARDEN FAIRIES...
ROSETTA, YOU DO KNOW WE'RE COMPETING, NOT SPECTATING, RIGHT?
HONEYDEW, WE'RE NOT GONNA LAST MORE THAN ONE EVENT!
IF I'M GONNA LOOK BAD, I'M NOT GONNA LOOK BAD!
DON'T WORRY! WE'LL DO A MAKEOVER ON YOU LATER!
!
RUMBLE AND GLIMMER, THE STORM FAIRIES, MAKE THEIR GRAND ENTRANCE...
WHERE THERE'S LIGHTNING...
...THERE'S THUNDER!
BOOM
WHERE THEY'RE GOING FOR A RECORD FIFTH STRAIGHT CHAMPIONSHIP RING AND EVERYONE CHEERS FOR THEM!

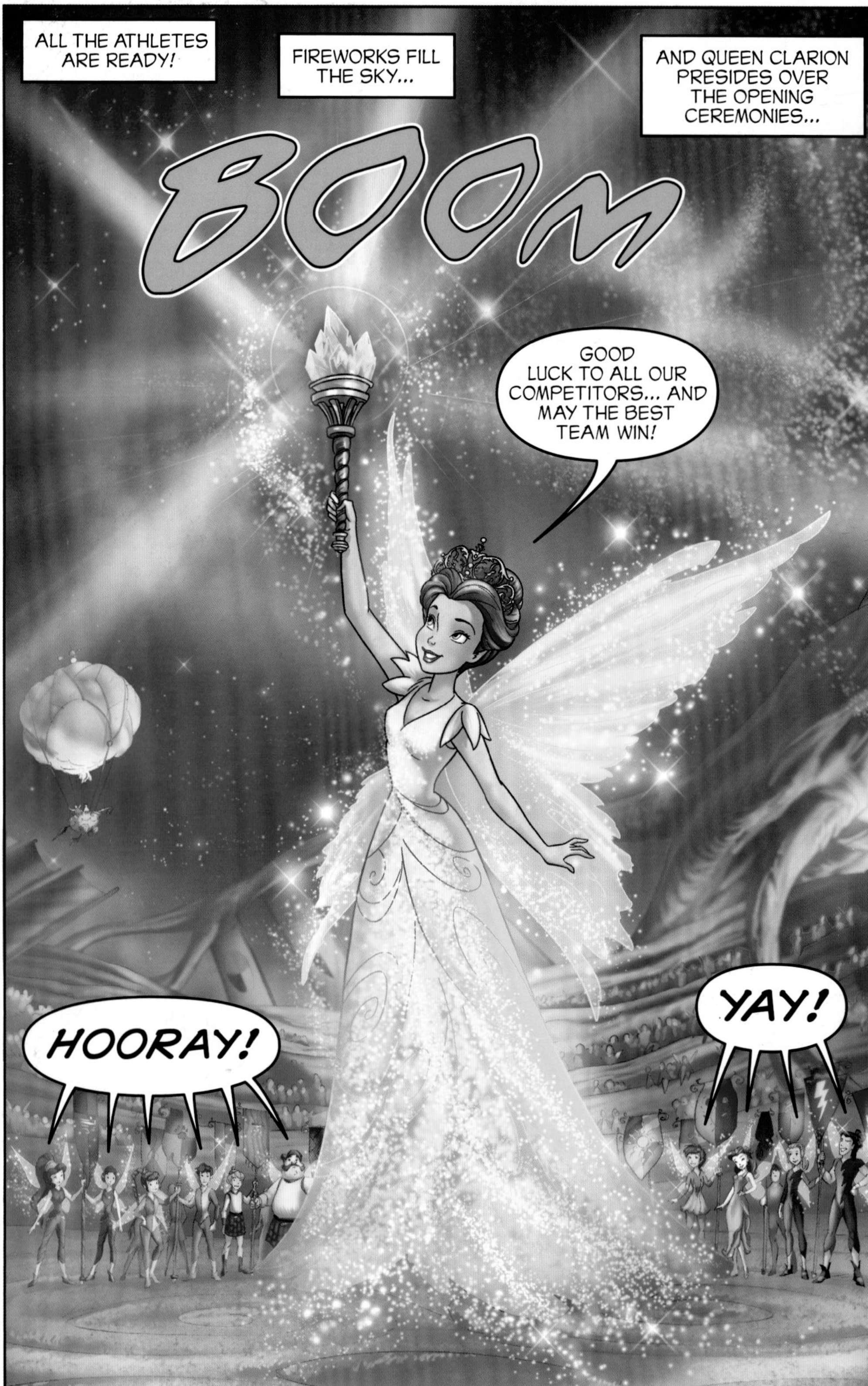
ALL THE ATHLETES ARE READY!
FIREWORKS FILL THE SKY...
AND QUEEN CLARION PRESIDES OVER THE OPENING CEREMONIES...
BOOM
GOOD LUCK TO ALL OUR COMPETITORS... AND MAY THE BEST TEAM WIN!
HOORAY!
YAY!

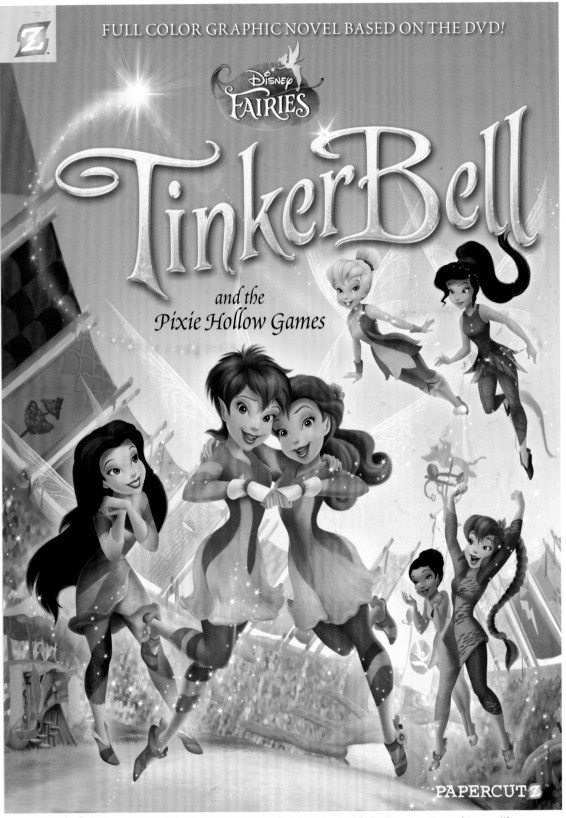

FULL COLOR GRAPHIC NOVEL BASED ON THE DVD!

TinkerBell
and the Pixie Hollow Games

PAPERCUTZ

Don't miss DISNEY FAIRIES #13 "Tinker Bell and the Pixie Hollow Games"!

More Great Graphic Novels from PAPERCUTZ™

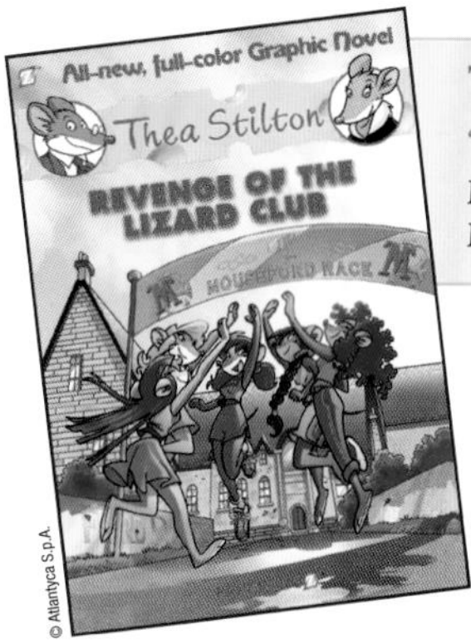
All-new, full-color Graphic Novel
Thea Stilton
REVENGE OF THE LIZARD CLUB

THEA STILTON #2
"Revenge of the Lizard Club"
Meet the Thea Sisters of Mouseford Academy!

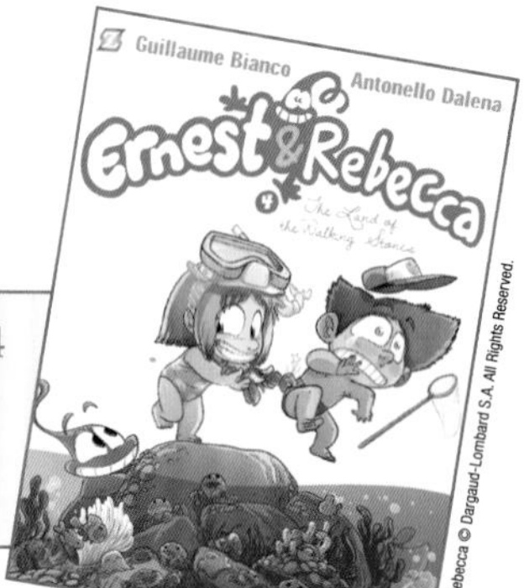
Guillaume Bianco
Antonello Dalena
Ernest & Rebecca
The Land of the Walking Stones

ERNEST & REBECCA #4
"The Land of Walking Stones"
A 6 ½ year old girl and her microbial buddy against the world!

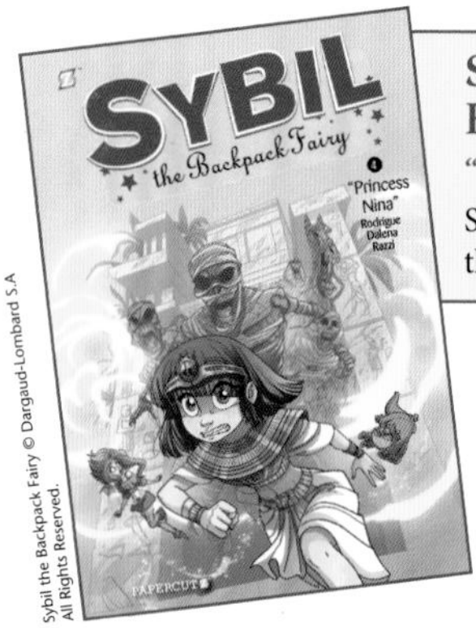
SYBIL
the Backpack Fairy
4
"Princess Nina"
Rodrigue
Dalena
Razzi
PAPERCUTZ

SYBIL THE BACKPACK FAIRY #4
"Princes Nina"
Sybil and Nina's excellent adventure through time!

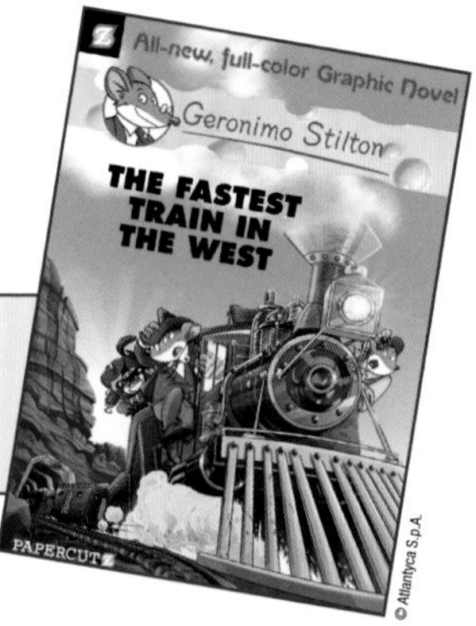
All-new, full-color Graphic Novel
Geronimo Stilton
THE FASTEST TRAIN IN THE WEST
PAPERCUTZ

GERONIMO STILTON #13
"The Fastest Train in the West"
Geronimo Stilton… cowboy?

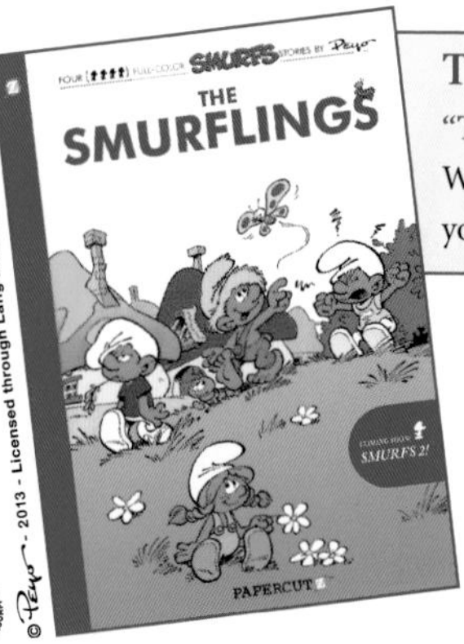
FOUR FULL-COLOR SMURFS STORIES BY Peyo
THE SMURFLINGS
SMURFS 2!
PAPERCUTZ

THE SMURFS #15
"The Smurflings"
Why are the Smurfs getting younger?

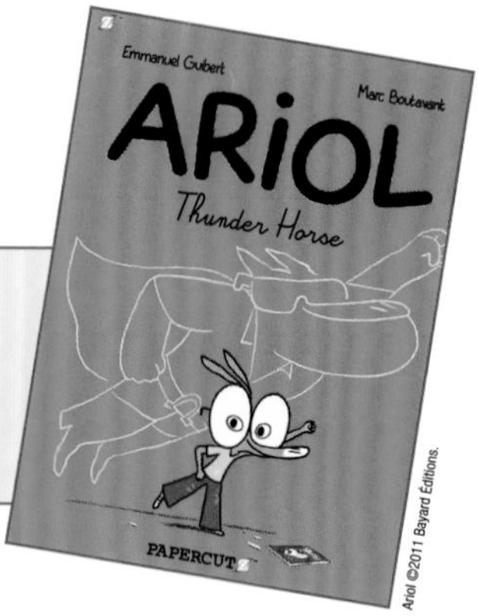
Emmanuel Guibert
Marc Boutavant
ARiOL
Thunder Horse
PAPERCUTZ

ARiOL #2
"Thunder Horse"
Meet ARiOL, a donkey just like you and me, trying to survive life at school.

Available at better booksellers everywhere!

Or order directly from us! GERONIMO STILTON and THEA STILTON are available in hardcover only for $9.99; ERNEST & REBECCA is $10.99 in hardcover only; SYBIL THE BACKPACK FAIRY is available in hardcover only for $10.99; THE SMURFS are available in paperback for $5.99, in hardcover for $10.99; ARiOL is available in paperback only for $12.99.

Please add $4.00 for postage and handling for the first book, add $1.00 for each additional book.

Please make check payable to NBM Publishing. Send to: PAPERCUTZ, 160 Broadway, Suite 700, East Wing, New York, NY 10038
Or call 800-886-1223, 9AM-6PM EST, M-F